"How are yo ~~ed,~~ **his gaze fin** ~~ning~~ **something i** ~~er.~~ **It's the home stretch."**

She should've been relieved. By noon tomorrow this nightmare would be over, but tension threaded through her. "My father-in-law begged me to take the money, keep my job at the firm and just forget everything." Lori almost kept talking, almost dared to unburden herself of the secret she'd been carrying.

"Of course he did." Nick clasped her shoulders with a reassuring touch. "Without you, there is no case. I'm sure the people they launder money for are dangerous."

A shiver raced through her. "Sam told me...there was no way to win. That I was going up against Goliath and they'd do anything to see me silence He swore I wouldn't live long enough to testif

HOSTILE PURSUIT

—

JUNO RUSHDAN

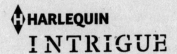

HARLEQUIN
INTRIGUE

To all the readers willing to take a chance on a new Harlequin Intrigue author, I am grateful.

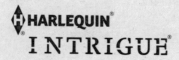

ISBN-13: 978-1-335-13643-5

Hostile Pursuit

Copyright © 2020 by Juno Rushdan

This edition published by arrangement with Harlequin Books S.A.

For questions and comments about the quality of this book, please contact us at CustomerService@Harlequin.com.

Harlequin Enterprises ULC
22 Adelaide St. West, 40th Floor
Toronto, Ontario M5H 4E3, Canada
www.Harlequin.com

Printed in U.S.A.

Recycling programs for this product may not exist in your area.

Juno Rushdan is the award-winning author of steamy, action-packed romantic thrillers. As a veteran air force intelligence officer, she uses her background supporting special forces to write about kick-ass heroes and strong heroines fighting for their lives as well as their happily-ever-afters. Juno currently lives in the DC area with her patient husband, two kids and a rescue dog. Be the first to know about new releases, exclusive excerpts and contests by signing up for Juno's newsletter at junorushdan.com/mailing-list.

Books by Juno Rushdan

Harlequin Intrigue

A Hard Core Justice Thriller
Hostile Pursuit

Visit the Author Profile page at Harlequin.com.

CAST OF CHARACTERS

Nick McKenna—This deputy US Marshal always follows the rules, but when a witness comes under attack, he's left questioning everything, except how much he cares about her.

Lori Carpenter—There was a price on her head the second she agreed to testify.

Ted Zeeman—Nick's partner is eager to finish his last assignment unscathed and retire.

Pamela Maadi-McKenna—The strong matriarch of the McKenna clan.

Bowen McKenna—As the eldest of four, he'll stop at nothing to protect his family.

Julie McKenna—She values family, fun and the right to bear arms.

Will Draper—Nick's boss is dedicated to the job, but is he telling his deputies everything?

Charlie Killinger—A member of the US Marshal Service tactical team and Nick's ex. Is she still holding a grudge, or can she be trusted?

Aiden Yazzie—Provides tactical support to Nick.

Belladonna—A ruthless assassin who has Lori in her crosshairs.

Chapter One

For a year Lori Carpenter had stayed indoors, under constant watch, cut off from family and friends and everything familiar, in hiding.

Dread ate away at her every day. There was nothing she could do besides prepare. But it still wasn't enough, and now her time was up.

The arm lodged against her throat tightened.

"You let your guard slip," he whispered in her ear, his elbow locked under her chin, blocking off her airway.

Her lungs strained, clogged with fear as she flailed.

"Show me what you are," he growled.

Prey or a predator.

Adrenaline shot through her bloodstream, her heart beating like a snare drum. Survival instinct kicked in and the lead weighing down her limbs evaporated.

Lori thrust her elbow back into his ribs, once, twice. All the drills repeated day after day for fifty-five weeks came rushing to the forefront of her mind. To break away, she had to flip him. She slammed her heel down onto his foot. As she shrugged her shoulders, she hooked her foot behind one of his legs, seized the arm locked around her throat and bent at the knees.

His body rotated, going over her shoulder. Perfect execution of the maneuver.

But he grabbed her, taking her down hard with him to the concrete floor of the empty two-car garage. They rolled. Their arms and legs tangled.

She landed on top of US Deputy Marshal Nick McKenna and jammed her forearm against his throat. "I asked you to give me a challenging lesson. Not try to actually kill me."

Nick was tough, deadly. There was a darkness to him. The kind bred from dealing in the worst sort of violence. She appreciated that about him; it bolstered her confidence that he'd be able to keep her alive. So far he hadn't disappointed. But there was another side to him she preferred.

He tapped her arm, giving the cue their self-defense session was finished even though he was lethally capable of maneuvering free of her grasp.

Part of her wondered why he had let her flip him to the ground. No way she could've tossed him unless he'd allowed it. Besides the fact that he was powerfully built, he had years of training and experience she couldn't compete with.

She took her arm off his larynx, put her hands on his muscular chest and kept his body pinned with her legs, straddling his hips. Her belly fluttered with raw awareness, so close to him, pelvis to pelvis, their lips a breath apart. He took up all the oxygen in the room.

Rubbing his throat, he stared up at her with those intense, bourbon-colored eyes that seemed to see everything. Her fear, her pain, her loneliness.

Everything except her desire for him.

His devastating dark looks were even more tempting dotted with facial stubble and covered in a sheen of sweat. "I'm pretty sure attempted homicide is not part of my job description." The overheated gravel of his voice teased an itch that hadn't been scratched in a long, long time.

He flashed a heart-stopping smile that sent a tingle shooting straight to her thighs.

"You were right. I have been too easy on you and that's not doing you a favor." He swept a long lock of her hair that'd slipped from her ponytail away from her face, tucking it behind her ear. The brush of his fingertips, his touch lingering seconds longer than it should've, made her stomach bounce as if she were still a naive girl who believed in true love and the magic of chemistry, instead of the older, wiser thirty-two-year-old woman she was today. "You need to know what the fear and the panic would feel like in a real-world scenario so you can *think* and *fight* your way through it."

Nick had been an anchor during the bleakest months, her sensei, teaching her to punch, kick, throw a proper headbutt. And he had become a dear friend. A smart, steadfast, sexy friend she couldn't stop thinking about crawling into bed with.

Ted Zeeman crossed the threshold, strolling into the garage while typing on a laptop. Good ole Ted always popped up before Nick and Lori slipped across the line of propriety, like he could smell their pheromones from the next room.

Lori stood and offered Nick a hand up from the ground.

He took it, putting his palm on hers even though he didn't need her assistance, climbed to his feet and dusted himself off. Standing shy of six feet with broad shoulders and streamlined muscles that hinted at his leashed lethality, he wasn't a huge guy, but his magnetic presence dominated a room. Or perhaps he simply dominated her attention.

She dismissed the ridiculous crush she had on Deputy Marshal McKenna. If she liked him, then beneath the suits and badge was a quintessential bad boy.

In her experience, bad boys equaled heartbreak. Every man she'd been attracted to had left scars. She wasn't in the market for another festering wound.

"Are you nervous about your big day tomorrow?" Ted asked.

Big day.

Weddings, funerals, your child being born…those were big days. Testifying in federal court against her in-laws' financial firm for laundering millions was inevitable once she'd discovered what Wallace Capital Management—WCM—had been up to.

After she took the stand tomorrow, marshals she'd never met would give her a brand-new name and whisk her off into a brand-new life in a brand-new city.

Hopefully, not one in backcountry nowhere.

"Yeah, a little." More like a lot. As in terrified.

"I'm about to file the morning report," Ted said to Nick. "Anything you want me to add?"

"Did you annotate our excursion?" Nick asked.

"Yep. You betcha." Ted nodded. "I reminded the boss, but I did the paperwork, too."

One hour a day, Lori was allowed off the premises. She usually relished the time jogging through the adjacent woods, but not today.

Ted slapped the classified US Marshals Services laptop closed. "I'm going to haul the trash out while you two get cleaned up so we can go *shopping.*" He rolled his eyes.

Lori might've been living in yoga pants, jeans and T-shirts since her mad dash out of San Diego after spilling her guts to the FBI, but she'd be damned if she was going to face her no-good, cheating ex-husband and his lying, criminal family in anything less than the best professional armor.

"Fifteen minutes and we'll head out." Ted tucked the laptop under his arm. "Tomorrow can't get here soon enough. My last assignment will be done, and I can finally retire."

"Are you going to get a little hut on a powdery beach like you want?" Nick asked him.

"Boy, I wish. It's a one-bedroom condo in the Keys for me. You'll have to visit."

"Better believe it," Nick said. "We'll be out front in fifteen."

Ted strode back into the country house that was isolated on two acres of land.

"How are you holding up?" Nick's gaze found hers again, warming something inside her like it did whenever he looked at her that way. "It's the homestretch."

She should've been relieved. By noon tomorrow this nightmare would be over, but tension threaded through her, tightening her muscles. "My father-in-law, Sam, begged me to look the other way, keep my job at WCM and to forget everything." Lori almost kept talking, almost dared to unburden herself of the secret she'd been carrying.

One stupid mistake had pulverized her life like a sledgehammer crushed a walnut.

It wasn't as if she could hide it forever. The truth

would come out in her testimony, but what would Nick think of her when he found out?

"Of course he did." Nick ran his hands up and down her arms. "Without you, there is no case. We're talking about millions of dollars a year. Billions. I'm sure whoever they launder money for are dangerous people and only care about their bottom line."

A shiver raced through her. Nick had no idea how dangerous, but she knew all too well. "Sam told me there's no way to win. That I'm going up against Goliath." And her father-in-law hadn't been talking about WCM. "He swore I wouldn't live long enough to testify."

The shiver deepened to a chill that seeped to her bones. The firm's biggest dirty client was violent and ruthless, had endless resources and people everywhere.

It was a miracle she'd lived this long.

"Goliath is big and ferocious. But not invincible. David beat him and so will you." Nick took both of her hands in his and held her gaze.

The gesture was small, but heated her cheeks and chased away her goose bumps. The space around them seemed to shrink, due to his proximity and the quiet strength he radiated. At times his tall, dark and brawny package was menacing, but he could also be…gentle.

"No matter what, I'll protect you and get you to court safely. Do you believe me?"

She believed he'd risk his life for duty and for any witness. "Yes."

Nick had kept her safe for three hundred and eighty-six days. What could possibly go wrong in the next twenty-seven hours?

NICK'S GAZE FLICKERED up to Lori's reflection in the rearview mirror of the car as he drove. Tension radiated from her slender body. Her expression was strained, her big brown eyes looking haunted. With her long chestnut hair loose and the flush of their workout gone from her cheeks, her fair skin was paler than normal. Somehow making the almost ethereal beauty about her more enticing.

The enormity of the transition she was going through wasn't lost on him.

He could tell she was doing her best to hold it together and not let nerves derail her. For a year he'd studied her. Paid attention to her body language and every nuance.

Witnesses tended to get antsy in protective custody, especially over a long period of time, and sometimes they made bad decisions. Tried to bolt when they should've stayed put. Deviated from protocol instead of adhering to the strict rules.

Buddying up to them helped him keep his finger on the pulse of the situation, anticipate if things might go sideways because an informant was on the verge of unraveling.

What he hadn't counted on was falling for a witness.

Lori had totally blindsided him. Several hours a day, seven days a week, watching her, talking to her, touching her during their self-defense lessons, was winding him up tighter than a watch spring. He'd never been so viscerally attracted to a woman. Everything about her excited him—her voice, those doe eyes staring at him, her silky hair he wanted to feel sliding across his belly, the knockout body he wanted to—

"Finally, we're here," Ted said, intruding on his thoughts.

Nick put the brakes on the inappropriate fantasy and leashed his raging hormones. Having an infatuation with a witness that bordered on obsessive was a reason to have his head examined.

He turned into the mall parking lot and pulled into a spot close to the west side entrance. The trip had been approved by their boss and planned for two weeks. He and Ted had gone over the layout of the shopping center numerous times, had memorized the location of the security station and every exit, and had narrowed down the mall's peak hours. That was why they'd chosen the morning, shortly after the mall opened when it would be quiet, no crowds and easy to control the environment.

They entered the mall through a side door and walked down a short corridor with a few stores. Only the tea shop appeared to be busy at this hour. An apron-clad clerk stood out front holding a tray of samples. An elderly gentleman with a salt-and-pepper crown, hobbling with a cane, approached the clerk and asked questions about the different varieties available to taste.

As they reached the central part of the shopping center, Nick was at Lori's side and Ted at their six behind them. The entrance they used was the closest to the women's business-apparel store that Lori had chosen in advance. The walk was a short distance, but everything stretched before him, almost in slow motion.

Nick surveilled their surroundings, noting everyone in the vicinity. A couple, one pushing a stroller, the other with a baby in a carrier strapped to their body. Three fiftysomething-year-old ladies power walking while engrossed in a lively discussion.

Nothing stood out or struck him as unusual, but there was a subtle tug of caution in his gut, like he was being watched. Another furtive glance around still didn't pinpoint any cause for alarm. Why his pulse pounded, and his palms itched, he didn't know. They'd taken Lori on a few other outings, although never to the mall, and never to the same place twice.

It was probably just the buildup of stress and pressure from his longest assignment drawing to a culmination with her set to testify tomorrow. They were so close to finishing this.

As much as he needed to keep Lori safe and get her through her testimony, he also wasn't ready to let her go. She'd been the sole focus of his life for the better part of a year. Resetting and moving on didn't seem possible. It certainly wasn't desirable. If he had a choice, he'd keep on seeing her, talking with her, hell, sneaking in a permissible touch—every single day.

But that was the one thing he didn't have a say in.

He brushed the thought aside, concentrating instead on what he could control.

They reached the women's clothing store. As they walked inside, a chime dinged from a motion-activated PIR sensor he spotted.

An employee behind the register, wearing a blazer and sporting a curly bob, made eye contact and gave a perky smile.

One female customer perusing a row of blouses didn't glance their way.

"Hello," the young sales associate said, her warm voice rich with enthusiasm. "Right now we have a sale on accessories. Fifty percent off. Let me know if you need help finding anything."

"Thank you," Lori said.

"You've got twenty minutes." Nick looked at his

watch while Ted swept the rest of the store. "We're in and out, okay?"

Lori went to a rack of suits. "You don't give a gal much time."

"One hour away from the property," he said, reminding her of the rules. "Not a minute more."

Nick's attention flickered to the other customer.

The woman was in her early forties, petite, olive complexion, coal-black hair pulled in a tight bun. No jewelry, wore slacks and a blousy top and carried a leather purse. She reached up, taking a shirt from the upper rack, and the frilly bell sleeve of her blouse dropped an inch, revealing a tattoo of a black rose on the back of her hand. The ink fit her. Beautiful. Elegant. Dark.

Reflexively, Nick pressed his arm against the Glock 22 in his shoulder rig.

"I don't see why I should be penalized because the house is thirty miles away," Lori said, checking the size on a navy two-piece.

The low chime at the front threshold rang. Another woman entered the store. Bottled-bleach-blonde. Tall and thin. Jeans and a buttoned shirt. Sneakers that squelched lightly against the tile floor.

"Eighteen minutes," Nick said, telegraphing with his hard tone this was nonnegotiable.

Lori cringed. "Yes, sir." She gave him a mock salute. "Have I told you how much I hate it when you snarl orders at me like a drill sergeant?"

Snarl? And drill sergeants were the worst. No one liked them. "You're exaggerating."

"Try understating. When we're out, you have two speeds. Icy cool and this Judge Dredd persona."

Nick realized he sometimes came across as abrasive when he was in work mode, but that wasn't the impression he was shooting for. At all.

She picked a suit from the rack. "This should work. I better go try it on. Tick-tock."

Nick looked to Ted, where his partner stood at the entrance of the dressing rooms. Ted nodded, signaling the stalls were empty and he'd make sure no one followed Lori inside.

Blondie headed straight to some dresses hanging in the rear of the store, grabbed one almost mindlessly, or perhaps she'd been in before and knew what she was looking for, flicked a glance at a tag and made a beeline for the dressing rooms.

Ted lifted a palm, not letting the blonde in after Lori. The woman huffed and protested, raising a loud stink, but his partner held firm.

Show her your badge, Ted, and be done with it. Flashing the Eagle Top five-pointed star had a way of shutting down any complaints lickety-split.

"Who do you think you are?" Blondie asked with a fist on her hip.

"A US Deputy Marshal, ma'am," Ted said. "Sorry for the inconvenience and the wait."

"Listen, jerk. I need to get in there now."

Ted laughed in his self-deprecating way. "Sorry. Not going to happen."

The sales associate went over to the scene unfolding. "Hi," she said brightly, her sunny disposition almost disarming. "Is there a problem?"

Nick maintained his position, monitoring the rest of the shop and the entrance.

Black Rose circled silent as a fox around to an ornate

display of scarves and ran her fingers across the silk. Not once since they'd entered had she acknowledged their presence in the slightest. Until now.

Her gaze lifted, meeting his, her face an expressionless mask, but her sharp eyes were those of a merciless predator.

Prior experience as an army ranger in Afghanistan before becoming a marshal had taught him the hard way never to underestimate a woman with a slight build, or even a child for that matter, and the deep scar under his chin was a testament.

For a chilling instant they stared at one another, sizing the other up. Not from a physical perspective. It was an assessment of will. And what Nick saw in her was fathomless.

Blondie threw the dress at Ted, dividing Nick's attention, and stormed out of the store.

The bell chimed. Black Rose's steely eyes narrowed before she turned and strode unhurriedly toward the door—as if she had all the time in the world.

Then he saw it. Her low-heeled boots that didn't make a sound.

His neck prickled the way it did when he was on a hunt for big game with his siblings. Nick followed. He had no reason to detain or question her, but something about that woman was *wrong*. From the tattoo, those rubber-soled shoes, to how she'd looked at him. As if she'd wanted to slice through him like a hot knife through butter.

None of it was evidence of anything and not cause for more than suspicion, but training and years of experience had taught him not to dismiss either.

The woman strolled away, lengthening the distance

between them with each store she passed. One, two, three. But the tightening in his gut didn't ease.

Black Rose glimpsed back at him over her shoulder, caught his fixed stare and stopped in her tracks. Pivoting, she turned and faced him, leveling her icy gaze his way. The look she sent him was full of loathing and in a blink it changed. Her lips hitched in an ominous half grin and she winked. Almost daring him to pursue.

Old ranger instincts urged him to take up the chase, confirm what his gut screamed about the woman, shake something that made sense out of her, but his training overruled recklessness.

He looked back in the quiet clothing store, checking on things.

Ted no longer stood stationed at the entrance of the dressing rooms.

Nick touched his Bluetooth earpiece. "Ted? What's your position? Do you have eyes on Hummingbird?" he asked, using the code name for Lori.

Deafening silence.

Nick's pulse spiked, but he remained calm—never one to succumb to panic. He stepped past displays and racks, his gaze scanning, his mind assessing.

No sign of Ted. Or the sales associate.

Drawing his gun, Nick hustled toward the dressing rooms.

Anticipation coiled in his chest, adrenaline roaring through him. The weight of his backup piece strapped to his ankle was a small comfort. Nick's fingers tightened on his Glock. He reached the threshold, scanned left, then right.

Ted lay on the floor beyond the entrance in a corner. Blood soaked his white hair at the base of his skull.

Son of a—

Ted was down.

There was no time to check if his partner was unconscious or dead. A commotion deeper in the dressing room drew him forward. Two people struggled inside the second stall.

The horror in Lori's terrified whimper jolted his heart.

Chapter Two

Lori's blood turned to slush, but her brain didn't misfire in the panic swamping her.

If she froze, she was dead.

If she didn't think, she was dead.

If she didn't fight, she was dead.

Lori had caught the glint of the door's lock moving in the mirror's reflection. But the sales associate had slipped inside the dressing room stall before Lori had registered what was happening or even had a chance to spin around half-dressed.

The next thing she knew, the young woman rushed up behind Lori and whipped some kind of cord around her throat. The sharp wire bit into her skin, pressing against her windpipe.

The pain from the instant constriction of her airway, the absolute terror, was mind-numbing. Her earlier exercises with Nick, despite how aggressive he'd been, paled in comparison. Deep down she'd known he'd never hurt her and that she was safe with him.

But the sweet-looking sales associate had morphed into a merciless killer and was strangling her to death. Every time Lori tried to throw an elbow back, the woman seemed to anticipate it, jerking her left and then right, spinning her in the stall as if Lori were a rag doll.

She fought with all her strength. Her attacker dug harder, not giving a second of reprieve.

Dear God! Where are you, Nick?

Lori sent her silent prayer up to some omnipotent being, the universe, to anything that'd listen. She was utterly powerless.

Her heart beat harder and harder against her rib cage. Her lungs squeezed as if caught in a vise, starved for air. She wasn't ready to die. Not like this.

She clawed at the wire tightening around her throat. Desperation welled in her chest. She tried to scream for help, to make any sound to draw attention. A guttural cry rose deep in her throat, but only the strangled wisp of air came from her mouth.

Her nerves ping-ponged as her mind surged for an escape. She kicked out, frantically.

At the same time, the dressing room door swung in. She glimpsed Nick for a split second before her bare foot—already in motion—knocked the door closed.

Pushing up and backward with both her legs, Lori sent her attacker slamming into the mirror. Glass shattered to the floor. Still clawing at the cord over her throat, her fingers slipped in the warm wetness of her own blood.

Her heart felt like it was trying to fight its way out of her chest, lungs burning for oxygen.

It was impossible for Lori to avoid the shards of broken mirror, and her naked soles were driven into the jagged pieces in the struggle. But only one thing mattered. Staying alive.

The door slammed open again. Nick used his hip and leg to keep it from swinging shut and aimed his gun.

He must not have had a clear shot because he didn't fire.

Lori's vision narrowed. Dark spots began forming in front of her eyes. Her panic-stricken heart squeezed.

Nick's voice rang in her mind. *Show me what you are. Prey or a predator.*

She had to do anything possible to give him a clear shot. *Right now!*

Lori threw her head back, smashing her skull into her attacker's face. Bone crunched and as the wire slackened a centimeter, she rammed her elbow into the woman's ribs.

With a grunt, her assailant's hold loosened enough for Lori to jerk away to the side.

Nick fired twice. The woman dropped to the floor.

Relief poured over Lori's soul.

Coughing, raking in air, tasting her own blood, Lori scrambled into Nick's arms.

He pulled her sideways against him. His hand clasped the back of her head, his fingers curling in her hair, and guided her face to his chest.

She broke down as sobs tore painfully from her throat.

"You're okay," Nick said. "I've got you."

The reassurance of his strong, solid form pressed close didn't do anything to loosen the knot of terror and anxiety twisting her insides. But she wasn't ready to put space between them. Not yet. She needed this. His warmth, his strength, his arms around her, a little longer.

"Nick. Nick…" she repeated again and again, unable to utter anything else.

She hated the neediness in her voice, the way she clung to him for dear life. Lori had never been a weak, whimpering damsel in distress. She took care of herself and never relied on others for anything. To do so only invited disappointment.

But this had escalated to the next level, to something that exceeded her deepest fears.

Someone taking a shot at her on the courthouse steps she'd braced herself for, but not *this*. Being attacked, nearly strangled to death in a dressing room with two armed deputy marshals within shouting distance.

How in the hell was that possible?

Oh, God. Oh, God. If they could get to her here, when her whereabouts and itinerary were supposed to be confidential, then they could get to her anywhere.

Panic swelled, building to hysteria. She was on the cusp of hyperventilating.

"Breathe. You have to breathe. Slow breaths, in and out."

Nick moved his head from side to side and she would've sworn his mouth brushed her hair. But she wasn't sure. Then his lips caressed her forehead in the barest touch, but the electric sensation was enough to burn through the mounting fear.

"I'm here. I've got you." He lowered his face to hers. His brown eyes—so authoritative and intense—anchored her. "I've got you, Lori. It's going to be all right."

NICK HELD HER tight to his chest, his heart sick with unfamiliar fear that threatened his composure. His muscles bunched, ready to blow a hole into anyone else who dared harm Lori. "Are you okay?"

She went limp against him, clinging to him with one hand and the other pressed to her throat. Her body shook so hard it was as if she might shatter into a million pieces.

He hauled her from the sight of the dead woman and inspected her neck. The garrote had left a laceration that would definitely scar if it wasn't tended to quickly. But she was alive and that was all that mattered. "Lori, are you all right?"

Nick needed to get her talking, make sure she didn't go into shock.

She sobbed into his shirt. Tears streamed down her face.

"Breathe," he said, gently. "Take deep breaths."

"If you had been ten seconds later..."

Brushing a finger under her chin, he tipped her face up to his.

Lori squeezed her eyes shut. "She would've killed me."

Seeing her hurt and distraught made his stomach clench.

Ten seconds. Such a close call.

How many seconds had he wasted focused on Black Rose when he should've maintained his vigilance? The woman had been a deliberate distraction, goading him, to give the planted sales associate an opportunity to strike.

He'd give anything to rewind one damn minute and prevent this from ever having happened. How had he missed the setup?

Nick was no rookie. He didn't make wet-behind-the-ears mistakes. The bait to hook his attention had been clever, well played. They'd been ready and waiting for Lori to arrive.

But how had those killers known they'd be in the store?

He longed to hold Lori tighter, closer, and soothe her, but this was the wrong place and the worst possible time. Once Black Rose, or whoever the hell that woman was, realized the assassination attempt had failed, she could come back—with reinforcements.

"We've got to get out of here." His gaze fell to her bare, cut feet and exposed legs. Nick ducked into the dressing room, glass crunching underfoot, and gathered her things. "Here." He handed Lori her clothes. "Get dressed. There's a med kit in the trunk of the car. Once we're away from the mall, I can treat your injuries. But we're not safe here."

More tears welled in her eyes. "Okay." She brushed loose pieces of glass from her feet and plucked at embedded shards, wincing from the pain.

Nick took a knee beside Ted and put two fingers to his carotid.

There was a pulse, thready and slow, but he had one. Thank goodness.

The possible horror of losing both a witness and his partner at the same time flashed before him. No, it wasn't something he would ever be able to live with.

He had to make damn sure that never happened on his watch. Not today. Not ever.

"Oh, dear God." Lori peeked around the wall of the dressing room at Ted's body while tugging on her jeans. "Is he alive?"

"Yeah. She must've hit him on the back of the head."

Nick loosened Ted's tie and undid the top button of his shirt. There was a lot of blood and no way to assess how bad his head injury was, not when Black Rose could pop up again at any moment. He hated it, but he had to risk waking Ted. Nick shook him hard. "Come on, Ted."

The old guy didn't move. Blood had trickled down, soaking the back of his collar.

Nick reached into his jacket pocket and took out smelling salts. As the middle child in a family of bounty hunters, he knew well enough never to leave without extra ammo, caffeine pills, condoms and smelling salts. Invariably, you'd need one or all of them.

He snapped the capsule of white crystals under Ted's nose, releasing the acrid punch of fumes. The ammonium carbonate tickled the membranes of Nick's nose and lungs, triggering his own breathing to increase.

Ted's eyes fluttered as he took a breath.

"There you go, buddy." Nick tapped his arm and helped him sit upright.

They had to get the hell out of there, but there was no telling what was waiting for them outside the store. Nick glanced at Lori. She'd mustered a brave face, her eyes wet with tears, but her stark vulnerability struck him.

"Take off your shirt," he said to her.

"What?" She gaped at him. "Why?"

Nick pulled off his jacket and holster and unbuttoned his shirt. Lori stared at his bulletproof vest. It was regulation for the marshals to wear one out in the field. The beefed-up hard composite body armor had an extra protection plate.

She caught his intention and did as he instructed.

Even though Nick had fantasized about seeing Lori undressed more times than he was ashamed to admit, he averted his eyes while he unstrapped the vest to put on Lori. There was no way to conceal the fact she was wearing one with only the T-shirt.

He reached up to the rack of discarded clothes, grabbed a lightweight blazer, ripping the tags off, and helped her put it on.

Ted held the back of his head and wobbled to his feet. "What in the hell happened?"

"We'll talk in the car." Nick roped an arm around Lori, leading them from the dressing rooms. "But right now I want us out of here."

BELLADONNA STALKED ALONG the upper landing of the mall, drumming her fingers on the cold steel railing. The clothing store was fixed in her sights.

Tension crawled along the tendons of her neck. She rolled her shoulders once to ease it, maintaining her cool exterior despite her nerves.

This was taking too long. Something must've gone wrong.

The two deputy marshals rushed out of the shop with the target sandwiched between them, shouldering past passersby down the walkway. The target looked like she'd been through the wringer, but the problem was she was still breathing.

Trixie had failed. The talented young woman could flip from happy-go-lucky to jamming a fork into your eye in a breath. She would be greatly missed.

Things had not gone as Belladonna had hoped, but she thrived on contingency plans and never accepted a hit without analyzing all the angles first. Not that she'd been given a choice in this situation.

Sixty contracts spanning over twenty years and three

continents had taught her it was far easier to eliminate a target if they were on their own or simply had a private security team. Mishaps were more likely to occur when the target was in the protective custody of federal agents. Preparation for any possibility was key.

With the main money-laundering mechanism of the cartel at stake, it was imperative to have layers of contingencies this time. A web within a web, and she was the spider weaving the entire sticky trap.

After she was forced to take this job, her employer had made it crystal clear that a five-million-dollar payday, her reputation and her life all rested on the outcome.

Failure wasn't a consideration.

She had too much to live for. A family counting on her this time. She had to finish this job. No matter what.

Gritting her teeth, Belladonna slid a steady hand over her flawless bun, ensuring not a hair was out of place. The store had been the optimal location to take out the target. A controlled environment. No witnesses. Disposal would've been simple.

This setback was irritating, but temporary.

What had to happen next would be messy, far too public, making it harder to contain and to clean up. The likelihood of collateral damage would escalate exponentially. Belladonna abhorred the unnecessary loss of life. The hallmark of a true professional, one of the best in her humble opinion, was no accidental casualties.

But it had to be done. If a little innocent blood was spilled in the process, ultimately it was Lori Carpenter's fault. All that woman had to do was keep her mouth shut. Would've saved Belladonna so much trouble.

Now she had to go through the hassle, not to mention the sheer inconvenience, of killing that bitch.

Belladonna inserted her earpiece and activated it with a slight touch. "Bishop, you're in play. No knight stands in your way. Secure the queen at all costs," she said to another person on her team stationed in a prime position.

"Check," the low voice acknowledged.

The only other thing she wanted to hear was *checkmate*.

NICK GUARDED THEIR REAR, ensuring no one got the drop on them from behind. They hustled toward their exit. The mall left them too exposed. There were multiple sight lines for a sniper to take a clean shot. He glanced around, trying to assess where one could hide.

No, no. He shook the thought off. They'd considered that at least. That was why they liked this mall. There wasn't a suitable position for a sniper's nest. But the shopping center did provide opportunities for a hit man. They hadn't factored in the possibility of an open, up-close assault.

The couple with the stroller and baby carrier looped back around in their direction. There was no movement from inside the stroller or the carrier.

Were the kids asleep? Or were those dolls and the gear a facade, hiding weapons?

He had to consider everyone a potential threat.

Two feet in front of him, Ted escorted Lori toward the last short corridor. Both were injured and frazzled and needed time to recuperate.

Lori hurried along with a hand pressed to her throat. The back of Ted's head was still bleeding badly. His partner might need stitches and hopefully nothing else. Ted was literally hours from retirement and had almost bitten the dust.

Nick itched to have his weapon in hand until they were safely in the car, but he'd holstered it after leaving the store.

The last thing they needed was to draw unwanted attention to themselves. Their scramble out of the clothing shop had probably already raised speculation among the onlookers, making them wonder if they'd robbed the place.

Nick spun on his heel, doing a quick three hundred sixty scan.

No sign of the woman with the tattoo. She'd vanished like a phantom. But that didn't give him a warm and cozy feeling, and it didn't mean there wasn't any danger.

Stay alert, stay alive, his former platoon leader used to say. There were no truer words.

They hit the west side corridor. The outer doors leading to the parking lot were in sight.

Ted held Lori by the elbow, keeping her moving at a rapid pace.

The older guy in front of the tea shop had progressed past asking questions to tasting samples. The nail salon and mobile phone shop were now a flurry of activity with customers.

A woman rummaging around in a large, bucket-size purse heading their way stole his attention. Nick slid his hand inside his jacket and gripped the handle of his service weapon, fingers tightening in readiness.

She pulled out a ringing cell phone and answered it, passing them by.

Nick exhaled the breath he'd been holding.

In fifty feet, they'd reach the doors and clear the mall. Then he'd reset from this epic disaster. Figure out how this could've happened in the first place.

All his senses were keyed up hot. Even his heartbeat had a machine-gun rhythm.

"I like the loose-leaf Dragon blend the best," the senior citizen said as Nick came within earshot.

The sales associate holding the tray smiled at him. "That's my favorite, too."

Only thirty feet to go.

The old guy pivoted, lifting his cane like a shotgun and aimed at Lori with shocking speed.

Taking him head-on was the only response.

Nick bolted forward in a rush and charged the guy. The AARP-card-carrier's eyes widened as he spotted Nick inbound and tried to redirect the aim. Nick knocked the cane up.

Bullets spit from the tip, spraying rounds on automatic. A plate glass storefront shattered. Rounds stitched up toward the ceiling. The air was split by the loud sewing-machine sound.

Ted pushed Lori up against a wall, out of the line of fire, and shielded her as he drew his Glock.

Bullets kept discharging in rapid fire. The gun concealed as a cane was such a thin, deceptive-looking weapon, but a stout recoil reverberated through Nick's arms.

The man fought Nick to regain control and almost succeeded.

Though the guy was older, he wasn't about to be put out to pasture. He had the strength of a bull and unleashed blinding martial arts moves.

Nick struggled to hold on to the cane through the assassin's lightning kicks until the weapon clicked. Empty. Nick threw a hard right punch, catching the older man full in the face.

To his credit, the man didn't stumble, but the blow stunned him a second. Maybe only a nanosecond before the man took a running leap into the air, screaming like a ferocious beast. AARP hoisted the cane up and swung it down.

Nick raised both arms, forming a triangle in front of his head to protect his skull. He took the brunt of the blow with his forearms and went for the man's knee with the heel of his foot.

The old guy was too quick and dodged it but left another body part vulnerable. Nick kicked the man straight in the gonads.

The cane slipped from AARP's grip and he doubled over in what must've been a world of hurt. But Nick wasn't gullible enough to think that man wouldn't recover in the next breath.

Nick grabbed the stainless-steel tray from the gawking clerk, letting samples of tea spill to the floor, and smacked AARP with the platter. A clang rang in the air as the man's head twisted. But he stayed upright, wobbling—still a threat. Nick threw his entire body into hitting the man with the steel tray again. Not once, not twice, hell, he didn't stop whaling on AARP until the guy dropped like a sack of potatoes and didn't so much as twitch.

Lori was safe behind Nick's partner, her face awash in renewed horror. Ted stood vigilant as a sentinel, determined not to let anything or anyone touch her, but his gun hand was shaking.

Not a good sign.

Ted was solid as a rock and Nick had never seen him tremble from nerves. Hopefully, his partner could make it to the car and Nick would tend to Lori and Ted later.

Right now there was a far more urgent problem.

The tingle in the back of his neck that slipped down between his shoulder blades told him he was being watched, and not by lookie-loo civilians.

He glanced around, barely taking in the carnage of broken glass and injured bystanders, bleeding and rolling on the floor from stray bullets.

One thing was at the forefront of his mind.

How many more hit men were there?

Chapter Three

Another bishop lost. Damn it!

Belladonna forced herself to stop staring at the target and turned, pretending to look at a storefront window display, in the opposite direction of the murmuring crowd that was gathering at the scene.

In another second or two, Deputy Marshal Nick McKenna would've sensed her surveillance and spotted her.

Unlike the older, softer Zeeman, McKenna was razor-sharp and capable. Traits she'd banked on in the clothing store when she'd lured the younger man away from the vicinity of the dressing rooms. She thought for certain he would've pursued her. The feral gleam in his eyes telegraphed his gnawing desire to do so, but he'd followed his protocol instead.

Something she bet he'd do again.

Even if she was mistaken on that account, she'd spent weeks planning, putting the pieces into place, waiting—down to the wire—for the final, missing element to fall in line.

There was nowhere they could go that she wouldn't

follow. Nowhere for them to hide. She had a carefully handpicked hit squad of more than a dozen left at her beck and call.

Belladonna whipped out her burner phone. First, she made a call to *housekeeping*.

"ETA on police?" she asked.

"They were just called," the whiskey-smooth female voice on the other side said. "A bystander in the crowd phoned it in. ETA six minutes. We've kept the mall security phone lines down and the video surveillance feeds to the clothing store and southwest entrance cut."

"Good. One less complication to deal with."

"You need to consider that someone may have filmed the altercation on their phone."

Exactly what Belladonna didn't need. Video footage slapped up on YouTube going viral. "I need cleanup. ASAP." She kept her own voice calm yet firm. "Two down. I don't want any DNA traces of my people left behind. Not a drop of blood. Not a single hair. No clothing fibers. Nothing. Do what you can to wipe the phones in the area clean. Are we clear?"

"As always. We'll monitor the internet in case any footage slips past us and pops up."

They'd clean that, too.

There wasn't a better housekeeping team on the planet, and they were worth their weight in gold. They would enter the mall disguised as paramedics and police officers, enabling them to move around unobstructed and unquestioned.

What they weren't able to get spick-and-span, they'd taint, making it worthless to forensics.

"Once you're done cleaning up this mess, restore feeds and phones before the media circus arrives."

Belladonna disconnected and sent a short text.

You're up, rook.

Standing by for a reply, she looked at the back of her hand and traced the lines of her tattoo—an inky rose. The symbol reinforced her resolve.

Tattoos or any identifying marks were a hazard in her industry, but she'd gotten it after her daughter was born.

The rose was meant to signify a fresh start, a path of her own choosing, a new identity.

Belladonna was the name the drug cartel had christened her when they took her in thirty years ago, smelted her down, trained her, forged her into the weapon she was today. It was Italian for *beautiful woman*.

And it was also the name of a plant. Every part of the nightshade from bloom to leaves to enticing berries was deadly.

Funny, she'd always loved the name and had embraced the purpose that had gone hand in hand with it until—

A response came back on her cell.

Ready to rock and roll. Set in ten.

She stowed her phone in her pocket. Lori Carpenter wouldn't live to take the stand.

Belladonna would make certain since her own life was staked on it.

"TED IS STABLE, and the bleeding seems to have stopped."
Nick drove the sedan, headed in the general direction of
the safe house, but with no confirmed destination yet.

His boss on the other end, Will Draper, would decide
their next move. Nick continued to check his mirrors
fifteen minutes later for any following vehicles. Using
the skills that he'd learned from his family and reinforced by the US Marshals, he'd gotten on the freeway,
gotten off and then immediately back on. Where traffic
was dense, he weaved in and out of lanes.

He exited for the state road that led to Big Bear Lake.
Rather than going to the safe house, he took a circuitous
route, looping through residential neighborhoods, passing the camping gear store and veterinarian.

At every yellow light, he shot through and made
sharp turns at the last possible moment. All the while
staying vigilant and looking in his mirrors for a tail.

"But he'll need to be checked for a concussion as
soon as possible," Nick said, finishing his update.

Until then, Nick needed to make a pit stop to get
his partner some ice for his head and to treat Lori's
wounds. He glanced at her in the back seat. Her arms
were wrapped around her midsection, hugging herself,
and her head rested on the window. A cloud of despair
and fear hung over her. She looked so fragile and on
edge and had every reason to be. He wanted to do something to restore her sense of safety, her belief in his ability to protect her.

The truth was he even doubted himself at this point
for letting his guard slip. Something that never should've
happened.

"Glad to hear Ted is fine. We've never had anything

like this happen," Draper said. "Are you sure you didn't pick up a tail at the mall? You're not being followed, are you?"

"I'm certain. We aren't being followed." The road behind them was clear, but he hadn't loosened his death grip from the wheel or let his muscles relax in the slightest.

"Good. I'm going to have Intel get to the bottom of what happened." Draper heaved a hard breath over the line.

Nick didn't know Draper well. Six months after Draper had been appointed as marshal of the San Diego office, Nick had been banished to the remote mountains on this long-term mission.

This assignment was a punishment. For losing his temper and communicating with his fists rather than his words with a fellow deputy—a real bastard. His boss paired him with mild-mannered, easygoing Ted, figuring the two of them wouldn't clash. An accurate assessment.

Draper's track record as an ambitious hard charger and reputation for positive results were well-known and had preceded him. Zero mistakes on his record.

"In the meantime," Draper continued, "we have no reason to believe the safe house has been compromised. Based on your location and Ted's injury, it's the best place for you to go. Far better than holing up at a motel off the interstate that could easily be breached. And the nearest hospital is thirty minutes away, not that you'd be in a defensible position there. At least the safe house is stocked with provisions and has fortified safety features in a worst-case scenario. Go there, enter with caution and stay put until I have further instructions. I'll call in backup."

The safe house wasn't a perfect option. There was no way to know what information the assassins had, but Nick agreed that it was their best bet, for now. A haphazard decision made from fear without all the facts could leave him and Ted exposed and Lori vulnerable to another attack.

"All right. I understand." Nick disconnected. "We're sticking to protocol and heading to the safe house."

Protocol was everything. It had kept the US Marshals from losing a single person under active protection in the witness security program for decades.

"Not surprising," Ted said. "Did Draper have any ideas how they found her?"

Nick spotted a gas station convenience store, pulled over and threw the car in Park. "Draper doesn't know how, but he's got Intel digging into it." A fresh wave of tension churned in his gut. "I'm going to grab some ice for your head. Keep your eyes peeled."

Ted reached over and grabbed Nick's forearm, stopping him. "I messed up back in the store." He sucked his teeth, disgust stamped on his face. "Let that girl get the drop on me."

Ted had a perfect record, stellar reputation and was one of the best to work with. Sure, he was about to retire, but he wasn't guilty of complacency.

"She was a professional," Nick said. "Looked perfectly harmless to me, too, and you were probably focused on the blonde as a possible threat."

The same way Nick had been focused on the brunette. Hell, he'd almost left the store to go after her, and if he had, Lori would be dead.

Ted grimaced. "Thanks for trying to make an old guy feel better, but I'll run in and get the ice. You stay with Lori. I couldn't live with myself if something else happened to her because of me. Don't let her out of your sight, kid."

At thirty-four, Nick was no more a *kid* than the assassin had been a *girl*, but Ted referred to anyone twenty years his junior as such. "All right. Two minutes, then we hit the road."

Ted gave a curt nod and climbed out.

Nick popped the trunk. "Give me a sec," he said to Lori as he opened his door, but she didn't acknowledge him with a glance.

He skirted around to the rear of the vehicle, grabbed the medical kit and slid into the back seat beside her.

She didn't look at him or shift his way or move an inch. Her blank stare stayed fixed outside the window, her limbs rigid with tension, a subtle tremble moving through her.

What he wouldn't give to make her stop shaking.

"Will Ted be okay?" Her gaze was still focused outside the window. "I feel awful that he was hurt because of me."

She was almost killed, twice, and here she was worried about Ted. Always showing concern for someone other than herself.

The more time he spent with Lori, the more he saw how she had a generous heart, one that he guessed had been hurt. He suspected it was the reason she was so guarded, but he admired her strength, too.

Tough as steel on the outside with a surprising vulnerability on the inside. An irresistible combination that had tempted him every waking hour in their close quarters.

Was the draw to her simply lust? Or something deeper, something more abiding?

The latter worried him senseless.

"Ted will be fine." He opened the med kit. "Is it okay for me to clean and bandage it?" He gestured to her throat.

She nodded.

Nick dabbed gauze doused with saline solution across the laceration.

Lori hissed, her pale face twisting in agony.

The last thing he wanted was to cause her more pain, but the wound needed to be cleaned. He applied triple antibiotic ointment to the raw wound and bandaged it.

"Hey, are you hanging in there?"

Another nod.

Ninety-five percent of the people the Marshal Services protected were some shade of criminal, endeavoring to evade prosecution by snitching on a bigger fish. That wasn't the case with Lori. She was a good person, a law-abiding accountant, no criminal history, who went to the FBI of her own free will. Most upstanding people didn't do that, believe it or not.

Turning state's evidence that qualified a person for WITSEC meant sacrificing everything. The vast majority weren't willing to accept a new identity without resources, credit or the promise of stability, all after being dumped in a strange environment. Their inclination was to look the other way instead.

While Lori's reward for doing the right thing by agreeing to testify against dangerous parasites was to risk her life, change her name, sacrifice her career, give up all her friends and accept a much lower standard of living. She didn't deserve any of this.

"Not much choice in the matter." She clenched her hands into fists, digging them into her thighs. "I refuse to roll over and give up."

Regardless of the horror and trauma of the past hour, she wasn't about to break. Her eyes were glassy from the strain. But beyond the tears there was determination. He could almost see her gathering her strength and he admired that about Lori.

She was a fighter. He'd seen her inner constitution during their hand-to-hand lessons.

No matter how many times he knocked her down or how hard she fell, she got back up. Sometimes winded and weary, but always with an easy grace, ready for more.

That took serious guts.

His mom had called her *incredible* in their weekly chats when he talked about Lori's compassion, her kindness, her courage—without mentioning her name or specific circumstances or anything to violate the rules.

"No. I wouldn't expect you to give up." Nick longed to touch her, as a man would a woman. Not as a marshal trying to put a witness at ease. He settled for setting his palm over her fist, and her fingers loosened instantly, taking his hand in hers. "But that doesn't mean what happened isn't overwhelming for you."

She wasn't a federal agent, hadn't grown up around a bunch of rough and rowdy bounty hunters, and had no self-defense training outside of what he'd provided.

This situation was bound to be tough for any civilian.

"I can't stop thinking about it," she said, her brow

furrowed, "when all I want to do is push it from my mind."

His fingers itched to stroke away her worries.

When she'd asked to learn self-defense, he'd jumped at her request. Sure, he was eager to teach her skills he hoped she'd never need in her new life, but it was also a tad self-serving. All their physical contact, no matter how brief or slight, how accidental or deliberate, had only stoked his appetite for more.

"I don't think the garrote will leave a mark."

"The gar-what?"

"The garrote. What the assassin used to…" That woman had gotten so close to ending her life. Too damn close. And that was on him. "It'll take time to heal. On the inside as well as the outside." Temptation won, and he brushed his knuckles across her cheek. Satin didn't hold a candle to her skin. His breath grew shallow as she leaned into his touch. "But I'm here for you."

He wasn't exactly sure what he was trying to say, but he meant as more than a deputy marshal. He *liked* her. He *wanted* her so much that he ached, and he'd spent too much time wondering what it'd be like to kiss her. But staunch professionalism had always drawn a fine line in the sand, stopping him from doing anything they might both regret. That, and the ever-looming presence of Ted, if Nick was being one hundred percent honest.

Not that he should be thinking about that now, considering she was still in danger, but he couldn't help it with her sitting close enough for her warm breath to caress his cheek.

Averting her gaze, she put her palm on his thigh. "You mean, here for me for another day, anyway. Then you're off to your next assignment, next witness to protect, and before you know it, you'll have forgotten all about me."

Forgetting Lori would be like forgetting being struck by lightning. Totally impossible.

"No matter what happens after tomorrow," he said, cupping her cheek, and his heart pumped double-time, "never think you were just an assignment or a witness to me." *Because you're so much more.*

Her gaze lifted to his, and something sparked between them. Warm. Undeniable. Stronger than rapport. She wet her lips, and he was tempted to hold her in his arms the way he'd fantasized for months, reeling her flush against him, and kiss her.

Ted came out of the store with a bag of frozen vegetables pressed to his skull and headed for the car. Impeccable timing as usual.

"I'll never forget you, Lori. Never." Nick lowered his hand from her face. "When we get to the safe house, I can take a look at your feet."

She nodded. "Thank you, for everything."

Before Ted threw him a side-eye, Nick wasted no time switching seats back behind the steering wheel.

Ten minutes later they arrived at the safe house.

Rather than stow the car in the garage, he parked in the drive. Better to check the house and perimeter first, proceeding with caution like Draper advised and his gut insisted on.

"I'll do a sweep," Nick said. "Make sure it's all clear."

Ted scowled. "I'll take point."

Was he kidding?

Ted hadn't tossed his cookies or lost consciousness again, which were both bad signs with a head injury, but he had a tremble in his hand and wasn't quite steady on his feet.

Nick was all for tenacity—they needed it to get through these tough assignments—but pushing it was plain stupid. "You could have a concussion. What if you get light-headed or pass out?"

"You're not leaving her side," Ted said, wagging a finger in Nick's face. "Got it, kid?"

"No, Ted. I don't *got it*. There comes a time when we have to acknowledge our limitations and concede. This is one of those times." Nick put his hand on Ted's shoulder. "It's no reflection on you or your record." He had admired Ted since he first started working at the San Diego office. A lifer who hadn't grown soft or complacent, eager to help the newbies, lend an ear of support and offer good advice when solicited or not. Ted was like the caring, helpful uncle everyone wished they had. "You're not well. You need to stay off your feet. I'll clear the house."

Ted looked back at Lori like he was reluctant to speak in front of her.

She made it easier by looking out the window and pretending she wasn't privy to their conversation. A small consideration that spoke volumes about Lori's generosity, especially in light of what she'd been through. She had every right to chime in, shout her opinion, accuse Ted and Nick of falling short and failing her. But she didn't, always one to take the gracious, high road.

"I was with Hummingbird when that girl got close enough to almost—" he dropped his voice to a whisper "—kill her. Somehow, I didn't see it coming. That's on me." Ted shook his head, mouth pulled into a grim line. "I've got the feeling that this isn't over."

Nick had the same queasy sensation rolling in his stomach.

Black Rose hadn't shown herself again at the mall. But she was out there, somewhere, waiting for the opportune moment to strike.

Would that happen when Nick left Lori alone with Ted?

His partner was injured, less fit and capable now than he had been at the clothing store.

Nick wanted to clone himself into an army that he could rely on to keep Lori safe, but he didn't have that luxury. He had to work with what he had and stick next to Lori. No distractions, no being baited, no entertaining any other possibility.

"You need to stay by her side and make sure nothing else happens to her," Ted said.

His partner was well respected, senior and technically in charge, but Nick could see it in his eyes—the need to get this right. No more mistakes.

Ted had made hard sacrifices over the years. His five tumultuous divorces were legendary. He wanted a committed, stable marriage and had tried multiple times to achieve it, and contested every dissolution, but this job demanded so much, sucked you dry. All he had left was his career and reputation.

Sure, it didn't keep a man warm at night, but he'd chosen to put duty first and accept the cost. Something all the deputies related to and commended.

To lose a witness was the one thing every marshal dreaded, but to have it happen on your last assignment would be a mark of shame none would be able to live with. Going down in infamy as *that* deputy marshal who'd lost someone in protective custody and becoming the focus of a lesson at the academy on what *not* to do.

No one wanted the torment of a tarnished legacy in their twilight years. It was all Ted had left.

"Got it," Nick said. "But if you start seeing stars, you let me know."

"Will do." Ted drew his weapon, switched off the safety and left the car.

As he jogged along the outskirts of the safe house, scanning the tree line of the surrounding woods, he did a quick perimeter sweep that must've made the old guy's head pound.

"All clear. Entering the house," Ted said over comms.

The security system gave thirty seconds for the code to be entered before sending an alert to district head-quarters and the alarm sounded.

Nick stepped out of the car for a better vantage point, keeping his eyes peeled for any indication that the safe house had been compromised. He trained his gaze on the woods. Nothing beyond birds and squirrels stirred. No tingle down his spine like they were being watched.

"First floor, clear." Ted's voice was tight, strained. Through the open front door, Nick saw him cross the entranceway toward the stairs. "Heading to the second floor." A minute later he said, "Good to go. Cleared to bring Hummingbird inside."

Nick opened Lori's door and escorted her to the house. The crunch of the gravel in the driveway under-foot echoed in the stillness. He ushered her up the porch steps, inside and locked the reinforced steel door capable of withstanding a battering ram. The house was stuffy, warmer by about five degrees he estimated, but the smart thermostat was set for efficiency.

After a small adjustment, they could all take a breather and recover from the morning. Gain their bearings and assess everyone's physical condition. Lori needed pain-killers and he had to examine Ted's head to see if stitches were necessary.

Nick had patched up a buddy or two in the field when he was in the army, a skill that had come in handy on more than one occasion, but he'd never treated a head injury before and wasn't qualified to try.

"Ted, what's your status?" Nick headed to the security system to arm it.

"Checking the crawl space in the attic. It's tight up here. And hot. But an ounce of prevention is worth a pound of cure."

This was why Ted was in charge, beyond seniority. The man might have a concussion, but he had the foresight and the fortitude to push through and check the attic. The assassins they were dealing with had proven to be resourceful and deceptive. On the off chance they had the location of the safe house, the attic would be a clever hiding spot.

Nick tapped in the code on the panel, activating the security features of the house, from motion sensors that would alert them to anyone approaching, to video cameras giving them eyes for three hundred sixty degrees. If necessary, with the touch of a button, steel shutters would deploy, rolling down over the windows—a cheaper, more efficient alternative to bullet-resistant glass—turning the shelter into an impenetrable fortress.

Each safe house was designed to hold up under an

attack and provide a secure environment where marshals could wait for reinforcements.

"Nick?" Lori asked, staring at the thermostat. Something curious in her voice tugged at him.

"Yeah." He turned, stepping up beside her.

"Look." She pointed to the Nest sensor.

He glanced at the round dial. Instead of the display showing the temperature, numbers were counting down. *Fourteen. Thirteen. Twelve.*

A raw, flaring pit opened in his chest as realization set in. The place was rigged to blow.

Chapter Four

Lori froze and blinked at the digital numbers on the thermostat rapidly counting down. The tiny hairs on the nape of her neck lifted. Her breath locked in her sore throat.

This couldn't be happening. One moment, the temperature had been displayed, showing seventy-four degrees. The next, Nick had set the alarm, and as she turned, she caught a flicker on the small screen from the corner of her eye.

Blind luck.

If she'd been standing at a different angle or two steps farther away, she would've missed it. But even now, her mind rejected what she was seeing.

Ten.

Her heart rate ticked up like a jackrabbit's.

Nine.

Oh, God. What was going to happen once the dial reached one?

A current of horror and dread surged through her, electrifying her.

Nick grabbed her by the elbow and hustled toward the front door. At the same time, he touched his earpiece. "Ted, get out of the house. Now. There's a bomb!"

His last word confirmed her worst fear. Echoed through her head on repeat.

Bomb. Bomb. Bomb.

A rush of dark energy overrode stark terror, blistering across her nerves. Her feet moved faster than her thoughts. Not that there was time to think or barely breathe.

Nick flung the front door open. A deafening alarm blared.

They were across the threshold in a heartbeat and burst out into the glare of sunshine. White lights mounted around the house that would've been blinding at night flashed at a frenetic pace.

Heart racing, she held on to Nick's arm, her fingers digging into him as they ran as hard and as fast as possible down the porch stairs.

She tried to estimate where the timer was by now. How many seconds were left?

Whatever the answer, they needed more.

Her pulse throbbed in her throat. Everything was happening at warp speed. But it was as if her limbs moved in slo-mo, not carrying her away quickly enough.

How big would the blast radius be? Would they be in it?

They were at a breakneck sprint the instant they touched the lawn.

Still, they needed to be faster.

She glanced over her shoulder. No sign of Ted. Had he made it out of the attic, much less the house?

The ground shook and a searing clap blew out the windows in a shower of glass, spraying wood shrapnel followed by a roaring ball of flame. The force of the blast sent them hurtling forward off their feet.

Nick threw his arms around Lori in midair, using his body as cover. They both went down, the hilt of his gun jabbing into her ribs. A wave of hurt consumed her.

They'd landed with him taking the brunt of the fall and most of her weight on him. Her head would've slammed into the ground, but he'd tucked her skull against his chest, protecting her face with his hands when they hit the grass.

Nick rolled, blanketing her. His strong, muscular body was as taut as a shield. She inhaled a relieved breath. They were alive. Barely. But they were both breathing.

For a dizzying moment she clung to him, her fingers gripping him so tightly she wasn't sure if she'd be able to let go. Lori's ears rang and her scrambled brain swam in a haze. Heat bore down on them, but her body was cold, skin clammy. She ached all over like she'd been slam-dunked by a bulldozer.

Agony rocked through every muscle, every cell.

Singed, smoldering debris rained on the lawn. Nick scooted upright, hauling her along with him. She was so shell-shocked the prospect of moving seemed unfathomable, but he yanked her from the grass in a sharp, urgent tug she couldn't resist until she was in a sitting position. He moved with such fluid quickness as if the explosion hadn't left him dazed in the slightest.

She sat, trying to gain her bearings. Her bones had been jarred by the blast. It was a wonder none were broken, but there was the sting of scrapes and scalding bruises.

Nick was on his feet, weapon drawn, scanning their surroundings in the same blink of time that Lori managed another cough and pressed a hand to her splitting head.

She braced for a squad of hit men to come storming out of the tree line any second.

When none did, Nick touched his earpiece. "Ted! Ted! Talk to me."

The sensation of the world rocking on a seesaw was subsiding, leaving Lori to deal with the pounding in her brain. She struggled to her hands and knees, finding the strength to stand.

Brushing hair from her face, she stared at the safe house, now engulfed in flames. Fire licked out of the broken windows, racing up the sides, tearing through holes in the roof. Black plumes billowed in the air. The roar of the blaze filled her ears.

Nothing could've survived that. Nothing and no one. It would've been impossible for him to have gotten down from the attic, climbed a flight of stairs and made it out of the house.

He'd been on the cusp of retirement about to start the next chapter of long, lazy days, fishing and drinking. Poor Ted.

Desperation elbowed aside her sorrow, putting her own predicament front and center.

"Ted!" Nick charged toward the house as if he intended to run inside and search for his partner.

A secondary explosion forced his feet to a sudden halt and his arm up, shielding his face. Lori's stomach dropped as she turned away from the blast, stumbling backward.

It must've been the propane tank at the rear of the house blowing.

Her feet froze, her legs trembled, helplessness swallowing her.

Nick ripped out his earpiece and let it drop to the grass. He stood there, daunted and gaping, looking as horrified and hollowed out as she felt.

Not once in the year she'd known him had he ever let raw emotion spill across his face. Every gesture, every expression, had always seemed so controlled, almost calculated. Like he never dared loosen the rein on his composure.

He hung his head a moment, shook it and then flipped right back into protector mode.

Turning to her, his face now inscrutable, he checked her over. "Are you okay?" His hands made quick work of patting her face and arms as he searched for any apparent injuries. "The shock wave from the blast could've caused internal damage," he said in a cold, detached tone. "Lori, are you okay?"

Aside from the fact that she'd almost been murdered three times in one day and it wasn't even noon… Aside from the fact their *safe house* was now a raging inferno, that everything was hanging in the balance—her life, her future, the prospect of growing old, all the things people took for granted every day like breathing… To boot, this nightmare was her own doing, and she kept making poor choices that turned a bad situation into an epic disaster. She had not only jeopardized her own life and Nick's, but also had gotten Ted killed. Now the only man left to protect her had hit the disconnect button and she cared more about whether or not he was all right than herself…

Other than that, she was just peachy.

"Nick, my God. Ted…" She wasn't quite sure what

to say. Were there any right words in this situation? She swallowed past the lump forming in her throat as he stared at her, his face a hardened mask. "I'm sorry. He was a good man and didn't deserve..." She stepped closer, hoping the frost in his eyes might thaw. "Are *you* all right?"

Lori put a palm to his chest, and it was as if the gentle contact flipped a switch inside him. The ice in his eyes liquefied into a dark, molten fury that sharpened the angles of his face. His features contorted into something monstrous and murderous, his jaw tightening. His hands clenched. His bearing held all the menace of a junkyard dog ready to tear into someone.

The hair-trigger shift in him terrified her.

"Whoever is doing this, whoever blew Ted to smithereens... I'm going to rip them apart limb by limb." He spoke with unmitigated gravity that left her speechless. "They're going to keep coming. Let them. Because they have messed with the wrong marshal. No matter what it takes, even if it costs my own life, I'm going to kill every last one of them."

PERPLEXED WAS A DECENT word to describe how Aiden Yazzie felt.

Watching Will Draper strut around like this was any other day, pretending that their office wasn't caught up in a CAT-5 crapstorm, left Aiden utterly baffled.

This wasn't about whether Draper was a good man or a bad man. Most people were a bit of both. This wasn't even about if he was making the right choices or the wrong ones. Everyone made mistakes.

Aiden wanted to know if the boss gave a damn.

Beyond how it affected his career. Draper was a fast

burner with serious ambitions, but there was something about him that Aiden couldn't put his finger on.

Everyone had their way of dealing with things. Aiden glanced across his desk to his partner and best friend without benefits, Charlie. She ran around wearing armor made of ice, acting as if the only thing that mattered was the job and kicking butt. He was all in favor of being a fearless female, but even Wonder Woman wasn't afraid to love.

Aiden took after his dad. Still waters ran deep, and on the surface he usually wore an easy smile unless he was ticked off. Or perplexed.

He turned back to the break room. Draper filled his mug with coffee and walked back to his office with his sunshine-and-rainbows swagger.

Not to hate on pretenses, but that nonchalance was totally unsettling.

Granted, Aiden and Charlie had the scoop on what was happening with Nick and the attack at the mall. The worker bees at Intel couldn't help but buzz whenever something went wrong. Pretty hard to ignore the drone of disaster.

"We need to make our move now," Charlie said, "before they do." She gestured across the office to the only other SOG—Special Operations Group—members in their district.

For this type of dire situation, Draper needed to send deputies certified as elite tactical operators. Most SOG members worked full-time assigned to US Marshals Service's offices throughout the country and remained on call twenty-four hours a day for high-priority SOG missions. Only toughies made of steel endured the grueling training designed to weed out everyone except the best of the best—not that he was tooting his own horn. Okay, maybe he was just a little. Once they passed, it still took someone highly disciplined to make a commitment to respond to an emergency at the drop of a hat.

The list of potentials for Draper to choose from was short.

"Come on, before Tweedledee and Tweedledum beat us to it," Charlie said, always hungry for action and keen to shoot something.

They didn't let their skills get rusty, training four days a week—Krav Maga, long runs, practice at the range—but there was nothing like the zing of a real-world scenario.

Still, a part of Aiden couldn't help but wonder if her eagerness was a sign that she had unresolved issues with Nick.

Why did she have to mess around with someone from the office?

Especially Mr. Dark and Stormy, who had that carved-in-stone jaw.

Eck! Aiden shook it off and pulled on a grin. "Let's make it happen."

They raised their knuckles for a fist bump and then touched their wrists together in unity.

Spinning out of his seat, Aiden was on Charlie's heels.

By the time Tweedledee and Tweedledum caught sight of them, Charlie was knocking on the boss's door.

"Come in," Draper said.

"You snooze, you lose," mouthed Aiden.

Tweedledum threw him the bird.

Aiden blew him a kiss and gave him an *up yours* arm gesture.

"Hey, boss," Charlie said, leaning against one of the chairs in front of his desk and folding her arms.

Aiden closed the door and turned. He dragged his gaze up Charlie's svelte figure, appreciating the sight of muscle where there should be muscle and softness where there should be softness. It was a wonder Yazzie was able to work around her without getting sidetracked and a tragedy he was firmly planted in the friend zone—*without benefits*.

Cursing Nick in his mind, he stepped up beside Charlie.

"We heard McKenna and Zeeman ran into some trouble," she said. "Are you planning to send backup?"

Draper stared into those intelligent, sharp blue eyes of hers, playing his cards close to the vest, wearing his usual *everything's fine* expression. "What did you hear?" he asked, neither confirming nor denying anything.

Baffling. "Assassination attempt on Hummingbird at the mall."

Draper shifted his gaze to Aiden. "Word spreads fast. I'll have to rectify that."

In all fairness, it didn't spread so much as it was harvested. Most of the office was still clueless. Take Tweedledee and Tweedledum, for example.

"Everything regarding Hummingbird is need-to-know. Who told you about what happened to McKenna and Zeeman?" Draper asked, his gray eyes narrowing.

She flashed that trademark, megawatt smile that was pure Charlie Killinger and ran her fingers back through her sunny-blond hair cut in an angled bob. "I have my sources and my ways of squeezing information from a person."

"I'm sure you do," Draper said, "but I'm afraid I'm going to need you to be more specific."

Her smile evaporated, mouth flattening into a frosty expression. "Intel is in a frenzy. It's clear something happened."

"We both nosed around," Aiden said, tagging in. "Heard McKenna and Zeeman were attacked and are going to need backup. This *is* need-to-know for SOG personnel."

"Then why don't I have all my SOG personnel in my office right now?"

Charlie tilted her head to the side. "Because we're smarter, sharper and better looking."

Aiden couldn't disagree on that point and threw in a nod for good measure.

It only seemed to irritate Draper based on the sour look that slithered across his face.

"Yazzie and I want in," Charlie said.

"No surprise there." Draper drew in a deep breath, slipping his composed mask back on. "Are you sure you can handle supporting McKenna?" he asked Charlie.

She stiffened, those sapphire eyes turning to slits. "What's that supposed to mean?"

Did she really want Draper to spell it out? Not even Aiden wanted the debacle rehashed.

"You and McKenna had a thing last year," Draper said. "He broke it off. You weren't too happy about it from what I've heard."

With a wave, she dismissed the assessment. "I mean no disrespect when I say this, sir, but any issues between Nick and me is our business."

And Aiden's, unfortunately. It had been this weird lover-lover-best-friend triangle. Aiden had had to hear about it from both sides. He'd played it cool and acted neutral, offering nuggets of advice that made his gut burn with jealousy.

And the kicker?

Neither of them had listened to a word he'd said.

"That's a load of hogwash," Draper said. "It became my business when McKenna got into a fight with another deputy over you, which I'm told you instigated. The issues between you two went from private to public with the incident."

That fight had caused long-term waves in the office that'd persisted after Draper had exiled Nick to no-man's-land for the use of excessive force.

Charlie scoffed. "Fine, let's clear the air and get on the same page. First—" she raised a finger "—Nick did break things off with me, but I was peeved because he beat me to the punch. I'm the one who pulls the plug on a fling. Not the other way around. Second—" another finger lifted "—I never instigate fights, but I'm more than happy to end them with words, and when that doesn't cut the mustard, I'll use my fist." Charlie stared at him straight in the eyes. "And third, I never allow anything in my personal life to get in the way of doing my job. Not ever. Sir," she snapped.

Aiden elbowed her. "You forgot one," he said to her in Navajo.

Fewer than a million people still spoke the language of his people and it was mostly only heard on a reservation. Charlie had taken an interest in learning when she'd accompanied him back home for his mom's funeral. Came in handy.

"What did she forget to add?" Draper asked, making it clear that he was no slouch and understood.

Aiden raised his brows and gave a nod that he was impressed. Because, come on, that was impressive and made Aiden even more leery of the dude.

"I'm quick on the uptake," Draper said, patting his own back, exuding that *me me me* attitude. "At previous offices I picked up a little Spanish, Russian and French. Call me paranoid, but I want to know what someone is saying in my presence."

Yeah, that did sound paranoid.

"She neglected to mention that Deputy Douche," Aiden said, refusing to sully his mouth saying the dude's name, "was talking smack about Charlie to Nick. She can screw who she likes and if she was a guy, that idiot never would've called her those foul things."

Tease. Whore. Slut. Aiden had made certain that every ugly, disgusting word had been documented in their statements. The other deputies had sided with Nick, Charlie and Aiden, and took to calling Jeff Snyder "Douche." Including the Tweedle duo.

After six months of constant disrespect, Jeff "Douche" Snyder transferred.

Good riddance, if you asked Aiden. There was no room for troublemakers on the team.

Aiden clenched his fingers to fists. "If Nick hadn't broken his jaw, I would've."

"I take it you would've broken his jaw, too?" Draper asked Charlie.

"Meh." She made a noncommittal sound and gave a one-shoulder shrug. "Sticks and stones. Right?"

"Okay. Fine." Draper raised his palms. "I take it you two aren't going to back down or back off until you get the assignment."

They nodded in unison.

"One question, sir," Aiden said. "How was Hummingbird's location compromised? Did the witness violate protocol?"

Draper squirmed in his seat, caught himself and stiffened. There was still a disturbing lack of consternation on his face. "We're not sure how the breach happened. It'll take Intel time to dig, unravel the knot of involvement and track any leads to figure out how we were compromised."

How an assassin had found their witness in the dang mall.

"You'll provide support," Draper said. "Zeeman is on his last leg, counting down the minutes to retirement of long, lazy days in the Key West sunshine. He's highly decorated, but short-termer-itis is real. Gear up, then head to Big Bear Lake and escort Hummingbird back to San Diego."

Charlie and Aiden exchanged confused glances. "Why are they way up at Big Bear?" she asked.

That was in the mountains. Hours away.

"I decided to use the LA office's remote safe house at Big Bear to keep Hummingbird as far away from San Diego as possible while awaiting the trial. Yes, it's an outside-the-box move. But I thought it the best way to ensure her safety. And," he said, straightening his tie, "Jack Foy himself commended and endorsed the idea."

Golly gee. The US Attorney for the Southern District of California himself.

Did Draper get tendinitis in his elbow from patting his own back so much?

"I'm going to call local police, or rather the sheriff's department," Draper said. "Have them send a car to the safe house and stay put until—"

Lynn Jacobs, Draper's assistant, hurried into the office without knocking, cutting him off. "Sir." Worry lines creased her middle-aged face and her watery brown eyes were wide with shock or fear. "Nick is on the phone. There's been another incident."

Chapter Five

"We lost Ted. The safe house was wired with explosives. He was in the attic and didn't have a chance to get out. He's dead," Nick said in a rush, as soon as Draper had gotten on the phone. He had to get through it as quickly as possible. Ended up stringing the words so close together they sounded like one run-on sentence.

He prayed his boss wouldn't ask him to repeat it.

"What? Are you saying the safe house was compromised, too? Ted... Ted Zeeman was killed?" Draper's voice grew more and more agitated with each question, and the underlying shock in his tone was to be expected.

Nick hadn't had a chance to process it, either. He gritted his teeth, still beating himself up for letting it happen.

Not that he saw how he could've prevented it. Unless Nick had gone into the house first and cleared it. Then he might be the one dead and Lori left virtually defenseless.

He took the resurgence of sorrow and regret, stuffed it in a locked box and tossed away the key. Reflecting on it, hell, relaying the details to his boss, conjured feelings Nick couldn't handle. Not if he was going to focus on Lori and keep her safe.

Nick needed to be impervious and driven. Getting bogged down by anything else wasn't a luxury he had.

The prosecution's hard evidence had disappeared bit by bit or fallen apart. Two other witnesses had flipped, and Lori was all they had left. Her testimony alone was enough evidence and would be the nail in the proverbial coffin of WCM.

Justice would be served one way or another, but in order for that to happen, Lori had to stay alive.

"Yes, sir. That's exactly what I'm saying."

"What about Hummingbird? Is she—"

"Alive. Scared and a little banged up. But breathing."

"Well, thank the Lord for that." Draper's relief was palpable over the phone. "But how, damn it? How did that happen?"

Excellent question. "I was hoping you'd have some answers for me by now on that."

"I wish I did. But I'm in the dark here as much as you. I have intel on it, scrubbing everything. It's complicated with the LA office's involvement, but our analysts will turn up something."

Eventually, they would. "But will it be in time to prevent another attack on Hummingbird's life?"

"Whoever set the bomb might believe Hummingbird was killed. Why would you expect another attack?"

Experience. His gut. Everything inside him screamed this wasn't over. Not by a long shot. "I have to anticipate anything at this point, sir. The bomber might've been hiding in the woods, watching for firsthand confirmation. We have to assume they know she's alive and will try again."

Draper heaved a breath like he agreed, reluctantly. "Okay. Where are you now?"

Nick hesitated, suddenly uncertain how to respond. He wasn't exactly in a hurry to invite more danger to their current location.

Draper had made the decision to put Lori in a safe house in a remote location, hours away from the support of their own office. A site that required sharing her whereabouts with the LA station. They'd been required to submit twice-daily reports, detailing everything down to Lori's mood and what she ate. Draper had approved the trip to the mall, knew the specifics of what entrance they'd use, which store Lori had planned to shop in and at precisely what time she'd be there. To make an ugly situation downright insane, Draper had sanctioned them to return to the safe house.

It was true that at first Nick had been bitter and, truth be told, furious with his boss over serving a yearlong sentence. But if he hadn't been banished to Big Bear Lake, he never would've gotten to know Lori.

Hell, who was he kidding? He never would've fallen hard for her. Something he couldn't construe as a punishment.

The grudge Nick held was long gone and had nothing to do with his current doubts about his boss. Without concrete proof that explained exactly how they'd been compromised, the compass needle was starting to point to Draper.

"Sir, maybe I shouldn't say. With everything that's already happened, it might be best to restrict any further details regarding Hummingbird."

"That's not your call to make, McKenna. I have a responsibility, an obligation to keep Hummingbird safe. If you take this course of action and deny me the ability to send backup, then you're endangering her and this case. God forbid something else were to happen, the blame would rest squarely on your shoulders. Not to mention, the US attorney's office might feel inclined to bill you for the wasted man hours."

Nick didn't care about taking the blame or being billed. If they fired him, he'd go work with his family. And if the US attorney's office was stupid enough to bill him, well, they couldn't get blood from a turnip, so good luck with that.

The point that stuck in his craw was that Nick would essentially be tying Draper's hands with regards to sending reinforcements. Something Nick unequivocally needed based on the morning's events.

"All right, I'll tell you where we are." Some techie in the office was probably tracking Nick's phone for a geolocation as they spoke, anyway. "But sir, I need to speak frankly. If any other hit men come calling, I've got to go dark." Ditch any means for them to track him and end all communication. No more updates on their location. "And find a way to bring Hummingbird in under the radar for the trial. I won't have any other choice."

"Watch your tone with me," Draper warned.

Nick had let his frustration tip toward anger and get the better of him. Lost the capacity for a quiet, civil tone somewhere between explaining his partner had been killed and trying to figure out if Draper had a hand in this somehow. He wanted to yell and smash things. He wanted to make the bastards responsible hurt and bleed.

Worrying about whether he'd ticked off Draper with his tone wasn't high on his list of concerns.

"Since you're such a fan of candor," Draper said, "I've got some for you, too. That's not your decision to make!" A string of curses followed. "You are not authorized to go dark. End of discussion. Now, I have two SOG operators sitting in my office at this very moment, ready, willing and able to assist you."

Tamping down the urge to punch the wall, Nick said, "We're just off State Road 38." He looked around the veterinary clinic.

His eyes glazed over the chairs in the empty waiting room, the displays of odor-masking candles and vitamin-enhanced treats that were for sale. The place was a glorified pet hotel.

Many of the upscale cabins and resorts around Big Bear Lake didn't allow pets, and folks wanted to board their furry, four-legged friends close by.

With no appointments on the books, it didn't take much to get the owner to close up shop while she tended to them. A flash of his badge. A vague explanation. Throwing out keywords such as *matter of life or death* and *discretion appreciated* did the trick. At his insistence, the owner had dismissed her two-person staff, lowered the storefront security gate—necessary for keeping local meth heads from breaking in at night and stealing drugs—and locked the doors.

"At Happy Paws and Wagging Tails," Nick said.

"What in the hell?" Disbelief sliced through his boss's voice. "Repeat that. Did you say you're harboring the US attorney's star witness at a damn veterinary clinic?"

"You heard me. Hummingbird had some injuries from the explosion, nothing critical, but I wanted her checked for internal damage to be on the safe side. I think you were right to steer us away from the local hospital." One good thing, but Draper's list of pros in this was woefully lacking. His credentials and reputation were solid, but something about this was thirteen shades of wrong. "Between the security surveillance cameras and their requirement to log the identity of all patients, we might be sitting ducks at the hospital. The owner here, Renee Holmes, hasn't asked for any identification and my badge has kept her questions to a minimum. Besides, this is the last place someone would look for Hummingbird."

At least, he hoped it was.

The safe house had been ablaze. Surely, the smoke had been seen for miles. He'd made a split-second decision to leave the scene. If someone had been in the woods, standing around waiting for first responders didn't seem like the wisest idea. He needed the most unlikely place where he could get Lori medical attention, and this was it.

"Nick, you've had a pretty intense morning, especially with losing Ted. It's good you're keeping your head and thinking clearly. Hummingbird needs you now, more than ever. Let the owner of Happy Tails, Ms. Renee Holmes, know that the US Marshals will compensate her for her services and that we appreciate her assistance. I want you to stay put. I'm going to notify the sheriff's department and have them send someone to your location."

"Please, don't do that, sir." Nick scrubbed a palm over his brow, struggling not to lose the little cool he'd regained as his thoughts raced. "I know that's a by-the-book decision and normally I'd be all for it, but too many people know about Hummingbird as is. We don't need to lengthen the list."

Besides, surely Black Rose was smart enough to monitor police channels. Zero in on a vague call to provide assistance to a deputy marshal. Even the use of something less transparent like a *federal agent* would draw the enemy's attention. Might as well broadcast the details about the witness in protective custody while they were at it.

Draper hemmed and hawed for a moment. "I see your point. Ordinarily, deviating from protocol is ill-advised, but I agree that an exception needs to be made considering the circumstances. Yazzie and Killinger are in my office now. You've been on speaker."

Nice of him to say something as an afterthought. Would've been great if he had mentioned it ten minutes ago when Draper had answered the phone. It was probably for the best to have others privy to both sides of the conversation. A lot had been discussed, an atypical course of action chosen and concerns expressed.

It was surprising to Nick that Draper had been willing to be so transparent with anyone else in the office. Then again, Nick had been at a severe disadvantage not knowing there had been eavesdroppers the entire time.

Damn. He tried to recall everything he'd said. Could anything be used against him later if things went from sideways to totally off the rails?

For the life of him, he drew a blank about most of it. But he'd been dead serious about going dark if necessary. As a last resort only.

"Hey, Nick." A smoky, feminine voice came over the line, the tone chummy-chummy.

Charlie.

"We've got your back, bro," Aiden said. "Hang in there, we're coming." Sincerity rang through loud and clear as a bell.

Some things never changed. After the hellish day

he'd had, it was Aiden who had shown more concern than Charlie. Surprise, surprise.

"They're going to suit up in tactical gear and head your way," Draper said.

Charlie's ice-queen disposition and Nick's quick temper were the reasons he was in this situation to begin with. He was no longer upset with her for not being able to connect in a relationship beyond the physical. And even between the sheets, something had been missing. Yeah, it'd been hot sex, really hot, but there'd been no intimacy. Like she kept her guard up even while screwing.

He'd thought the mention of her name, hearing her voice, would raise a bunch of messy, conflicted emotions, but maybe time did heal all wounds. He felt absolutely nothing besides relief. Charlie and Aiden were both formidable, the epitome of warriors, and he couldn't name anybody else from the office he'd rather have at his side at a time like this.

"And I'm going to request to have a full SOG unit at the courthouse tomorrow," Draper said. "In the meantime, catch your breath and rest up if you can."

"Got it," Nick said. "We'll be waiting."

Draper disconnected and Nick put his phone away in his pocket.

He went to the bathroom, splashed cold water on his face, and stared in the mirror.

Crap. He looked like canned dog food warmed over—felt like it, too. What he wouldn't give for a stiff drink to take the edge off.

Nick dried his face with paper towels and went to check on Lori in the back. Most of the dogs in the nearby kennels that were stacked along the wall responded to his presence. Some barked and yipped. A few panted and wagged their tails. Others simply stared at him.

Passing the cages, he spotted the open door to exam room two. Lori was right where he'd left her, sitting on a steel table.

This time, the body armor that had *US Marshals Service* written across the front had been discarded in a chair, her neck properly bandaged, and her scrapes and bruises had been treated and dressed down to her feet.

"Twenty-eight is pretty young to have your own veterinary clinic," Lori said.

"Technically, the place isn't mine. It belongs to Dr. Nguyen. I started interning when I was sixteen. When I finished my residency here, he just stopped coming in and let me take over. He spends all his time up at the lake now."

Nick stepped into the doorway.

"All done patching her up," Dr. Holmes said. "She doesn't have any broken bones, no internal injuries and no concussion."

Lori glanced up at him. The same wariness that had shone in her eyes when he'd ranted and raved like a complete psychopath about tearing people apart limb by limb was still there.

He'd let the darkest, ugliest part of himself show. A side few outside of his family had seen and lived to talk about. His gut churned at what she must think of him.

Lori lowered her eyes and wrung her hands.

"She's lucky," Nick said, "considering what we've been through."

Dr. Holmes sent him a sad smile. "Although I'm not

privy to the specifics, I gather it's a doozy. Would you like me to examine you, as well?"

"You've been so kind, Dr. Holmes. I wouldn't want to impose further and put you through the trouble."

"It's Renee, and it's no trouble in the slightest. I don't mind. Not every day I get human patients, you know."

"Thank you, but..." Nick shook his head. "Do you mind if we stay here a few hours?"

"Would I have to keep the clinic closed?"

"Yes. You would."

"What's a few hours?" Renee asked.

"Two to three. I have backup coming, tactical certified marshals, but they're on their way from San Diego. I know it's a big inconvenience. The Marshals Service will compensate you for your time."

"Money isn't the issue. I have to say this, otherwise, I'll kick myself later if I don't," Renee said. "I get the impression you two are running from something. I know this isn't my lane of expertise, but why don't you call the local authorities to help you?" Healthy suspicion crossed her face. "Wait for your friends to arrive at the sheriff's department instead of here. Unless whatever you're doing isn't legal."

The question and her supposition were both legitimate. Guess it was only a matter of time before he had to give her some real answers.

"I'm being hunted," Lori said.

Renee reeled back in surprise.

"I'm the material witness for an important case. There are a lot of people who don't want me to testify."

"Oh, hon." Renee clasped her shoulder, gave it a sympathetic squeeze and lowered her hand. "With you being a deputy marshal and the two of you showing up looking like you'd just been through World War Three, I figured it was something like that. But it doesn't really answer my question." She gave Nick a pointed look.

"No, it doesn't. My office was breached. Compromised somehow. At this point, the more people who know about her," Nick said, gesturing to Lori, "and her whereabouts, the harder it'll be to protect her. I don't know the sheriff around here or if he's got any crooked deputies in his office who might be willing to sell information. The people chasing her would pay a lot to get their hands on her."

"She. Not he. The sheriff is my mother and I know the three deputies that work for her. We grew up together. One of them is my cousin. They are honorable, good, trustworthy people. I'm talking salt of the earth. They'll help protect her until your tactical reinforcements arrive. I can't stay closed for three hours. One of the deputies will pass by in that time span and know something is wrong. So either you let me call my mom and ask her to come discreetly, no details over the phone, and you two can work it out in person, or you have to find someplace else to lay low until your friends show up."

Why couldn't anything be simple? "Do you mind giving us a moment?"

"Not at all." Renee tossed bloodied gauze in the trash and washed her hands. "I'll give you two some space to talk and decide. It's treat time for my buddies, anyway." The doctor went to shut the door.

"Please leave it open," Nick said. "Thank you."

He trusted the doctor. Sort of. She was a good-natured woman who only seemed to care about helping animals and people, but he'd prefer to know what the doctor was up to while they were in the clinic. So many unforeseen things had happened.

Renee nodded and left them alone.

Nick ducked his head into the hallway. Dr. Holmes grabbed a container of treats and went straight to the cages. All the dogs got excited, wagging their tails and jumping up on the metal doors.

Satisfied the doctor wasn't up to anything nefarious, he turned back to Lori.

Her coffee-colored eyes met his. Familiar desire to draw nearer and comfort her squeezed his chest, driving his feet toward her.

She hugged herself, hands gripping her elbows like she was afraid of him getting too close.

A wall seemed to lift between them. The one that had taken her months to lower before she had relaxed around him, started smiling, tossing out jokes, letting her humor and warmth shine. Gifting him with the pleasure of her laughter. There was no sweeter sound.

Nick stood still, hating himself for the way he'd lost control in front of her.

"What are we going to do?" Lori asked, averting her gaze.

"The idea of involving another office in this doesn't sit well with me. It could open a whole new can of worms. But if the sheriff and her deputies are truly as Renee described," he said, knowing they sounded a little too good to be true, "and her mother is willing to keep quiet about your presence, then we'd be ten times safer there than sitting at a restaurant."

"Okay. Whatever you think is best." She wrung her hands again and opened her mouth to say something else. A tense, silent moment passed, and she pressed her lips shut.

"Lori," he said, thankful that with the enthusiastic yelps in the other room the doctor couldn't overhear their conversation even though the door was open. "I'm sorry if I scared you out there with the things I said." He looked down at his field boots for a moment and then back up at her. "I was furious, and I spoke without thinking. I just want to reassure you that you're safe with me." When she didn't respond, he added, "I'll let Renee know our decision and leave you alone." He edged toward the door, his hands tightening at his sides.

"Nick, wait."

Chapter Six

"I don't want to be alone," Lori said.

As much as Nick wanted to believe that, her body language said otherwise. "Clearly, I'm making you uncomfortable."

"You did scare me out there. Seeing that side of you." She dropped her arms and scrubbed her palms on her thighs. "But I'm not afraid of you and you're not making me uncomfortable."

He gritted his teeth at that guarded glint in her eyes. "I can tell just by being in the same room that I'm making you uneasy. You have every right to be after my outburst. I don't blame you. I'm sorry you had to see me like that." *Completely unglued. Way to show self-control.*

"I wanted to talk to you about everything. What you said out there. I was nervous because I didn't know how to bring it up without you feeling judged and that's the last thing I want."

He slipped his hands in his pockets. "Look, you're fighting for your life. Judgment is natural. The dark place I have to go to sometimes is a hazard of the trade, but you shouldn't have to worry about the person assigned to protect you." *And whether I'm a raging lu-*

natic who is two seconds away from snapping. "I lost it out there. Said stuff that shouldn't have been said. It was unprofessional."

"I'm glad you voiced your thoughts. Relieved you brought it up first. The men that have been in my life have tended to hide who they really are until I'm in deep and then they sprang their inner monster on me. I've been on that nauseating merry-go-round so many times I've come to expect it. But that's not what I want." She slid down from the table to her bare feet that'd been bandaged and winced, staying an arm's reach away. "You hold back so much of yourself with me sometimes, but I knew there was more to you than what you were showing me. I'd rather see it all up front. Even the parts that might terrify me. So don't hold anything back. At least that way I know who and what I'm really dealing with."

She was asking for honesty. Something he could handle. Something he could give.

He closed the distance between them. On impulse, he took her hand, then thought better of it and let go. "Leaving the army wasn't my choice. I was discharged, honorably only because my commanding officer saw fit to show me leniency. I killed an enemy combatant in custody."

Lori gripped the steel table behind her but didn't look away from him. "Was it an accident?" Her tone was quiet, gentle.

This was what he'd wanted from Charlie and she'd been unable to give. Care and concern as she showed genuine interest in him, asking the tough questions.

Now that he was getting it from Lori, he wasn't sure he liked it. No telling how she'd respond once she heard the answer.

"No. Not an accident." Didn't get more deliberate than what he'd done. "It wasn't premeditated, but JAG would've had legitimate cause to charge me with manslaughter, if not for my CO's intervention. The prisoner was trying to escape and while doing so, he murdered several people. One was this young contractor who'd worked in the kitchen. She was pregnant and scheduled to be sent back home in a week. But she was in the wrong place at the wrong time. When I caught him, I was enraged." Nick hesitated, deliberating whether to stop there or let her know precisely what he was capable of. "I bashed his skull in, against a brick wall." Saying the words aloud sounded just as horrific as his memory of that night.

Sharing it with her, he never felt more vulnerable than at that moment.

He took a deep breath, still ashamed of his actions, embracing the familiar pain and disappointment that flowed whenever he thought about it.

Deep down, Nick believed in justice. It was the reason he became a marshal. The balance of the scales and making the punishment fit the crime. What he'd done in Afghanistan had been a frenzied act of vengeance.

Sometimes the lines blurred. Sometimes he went too far. Sometimes he wondered, at his core, if he was a good man who did bad things for the right reason, or if he was simply rotten.

Watching Lori, he waited for the look of disgust to cross her face. Waited for the rejection.

It didn't come.

Maybe Lori's heart was so big and generous that she excused his eruption at the safe house and his confession surrounding his discharge from the army, but there was more.

Three strikes and she'd have to wash her hands of him. Accept that his inner monster was beyond redemption.

"I was given this assignment to protect you as a punishment. My boss, Draper, wanted to remove me from the home office because I got into a fight with another deputy and used excessive force. I broke his jaw. He had to have it wired and was in a lot of pain for a long time."

Sufficient time for that jerk to reflect and regret the things that he had said. Hopefully, he'd never talk about another colleague in the same disrespectful manner that he had used with Charlie.

Still, Nick had crossed the line. He owned that and took responsibility for his actions.

"The deputy, whose jaw you broke. Did he deserve it?" she asked.

Hell, yeah. "I should've used my head, not let emotion get the better of me, and shown more self-control."

She released the table and shifted closer. "In Afghanistan, your commanding officer protected you. Not only from being brought up on charges, but also from being given a dishonorable discharge."

He shrugged. "I got lucky. That's all." Different leadership could've led to a different outcome. One with him in an orange jumpsuit at Fort Leavenworth.

"Draper didn't fire you or suspend you for a reason, and it wasn't luck. This case I'm supposed to testify in is big."

Huge. *Major.* US Attorney Foy planned to use the win as a platform to run for governor.

"Yet, they put my life in your hands." She stroked

a finger between his eyebrows as if to smooth out the worry line, and caressed his cheek. "What I saw in you at the safe house, the aggression, the thirst for violence, that's precisely what's going to give me the best chance to survive. Don't ever apologize for being who you are. I'm still breathing because of you."

Those words hit him dead center, healing something inside him that he hadn't realized was broken. She didn't see him as a monster. Lori wasn't afraid of him.

The weight of shame lifted, leaving him lighter. Liberated.

No woman had ever seen that side of him and understood it for what it was, trusted he'd never turn that darkness on her. Shown him affection in return. Lori was the first.

Forget professionalism and protocol. Overlook the fact that she was a witness, an assignment. Lori tempted him like no other.

Right or wrong, he wanted her with an aching need that was wearing down his restraint.

She reached for his hand, drew it to her chest and held it in place. The gesture wasn't provocative but intimate, deepening the connection between them. Her gaze flickered down to his mouth and then back up to his eyes.

"You're like an onion, Nick McKenna—lots of layers. Some of them pretty dark. But I've got a funny feeling about you."

"Oh, yeah? What's that?"

"No matter how deep or scary those layers are, I don't think you'd make me cry."

THE AIR HUNG thick between them, electrified, damn near flammable, and they were two pieces of flint, igniting whenever they touched. One tiny spark and they might both combust.

"I would never make you cry," he said. "Unless they were happy tears. You're such a good person, so beautiful. I'd cut off my right arm before hurting you."

On some level, despite his bad-boy alter ego, she sensed he believed that to be true.

"What about you?" He caressed her cheek with his knuckles, those dark, exacting eyes taking her in. "You've been holding back pieces of yourself, too." A statement, not a question, that stalled the oxygen in her lungs. "I just shared my darkest, ugliest secrets. Quid pro quo."

The caress in his voice was more powerful than a physical stroke, tempting her to unburden herself. Nick was formidable and capable. He could handle anything.

Even the truth?

Don't be so naive.

She tensed and backed up against the table. If he knew... No, when he found out...

Lori wasn't ready for that, to ruin this precious moment. "What you see is what you get with me."

Nick flashed her a *come on* look and erased the gap separating them. "We all have secrets."

Sins to atone for. But hers wasn't wrath. Or up for discussion.

"You're safe with me, Lori," he said, and she knew he didn't only mean physically, but her heart was battered and bruised, more fragile than she dared admit.

He slid his hand under her hair at the nape, cupping the back of her head, and dragged her flush against him. Lori's body heated and her pulse kicked up at his proximity.

She didn't resist, surrendering to his maleness and sexiness and the take-charge side of him, the blend of which was intoxicating.

His strong arm wrapped around her waist. Protectively at first, then he planted his palm on the small of her back in possession, drawing her pelvis to his. Her gaze moved past his broad shoulders and fixed on his lips. He looked like the kind of guy who kissed and made love the way that he fought. No holds barred, pouring his all into it.

Life was too short. The god-awful events of the day had made her painfully aware of that, more than ever. She was done holding back, tired of denying her growing attraction to this man.

"All I've wanted since the day I was assigned to you," he said, "was to protect you, keep you safe." That smoldering gaze searched hers and she was tempted to confess everything.

He was a little dark, a little crazy, a little rough. Dangerous, but the good kind. She was a little damaged, a little pragmatic and a whole lot scared. Dangerous, too, but a different sort.

They were wrong for each other in a thousand ways.

Knowing there was no future for them, but having such powerful chemistry, it was impossible to be rational.

"Is that all you've wanted over the past year?"

She didn't want to die with regrets. Wishing she had seized the chance to taste Nick McKenna, just once. Her mouth watered at the thought. She'd never been so hungry for a man's kiss, for his touch.

"No. It's not." He fell silent then and cupped her cheek. His thumb brushed over her lower lip like a breath and caused a liquid rush of weakness in her knees.

He gripped her hips, lifting her up onto the table, and pushed forward. She let her legs slide apart to accommodate him.

"I've wanted *you* since I first touched you." He squeezed his eyes shut, an intensity she'd never seen in him taking over his features. "Those self-defense lessons, the grappling, the holds, my wandering mind taking me places it shouldn't go, the excuses to put my hands on you without enjoying you the way I secretly wanted was—" he broke off, bringing his face close, and finished in a rough voice "—pure torture."

His admission left her breathless, speechless, but her belly tightened and rolled in response. Nick McKenna had desired her all this time. She exhaled in relief and moistened her lips.

He pressed his forehead to hers and opened his eyes. Their gazes collided.

Her muscles strained with anticipation. The urge to hasten the contact that she craved swelled in her chest like a soap bubble and she had to act before it burst.

In the span of a breath, her arms twined around his neck and her lips were on his. The kiss was shockingly soft at first, closemouthed and languid.

His tongue glided along the seam of her mouth, teasing it open. She melted against him and sighed as his grip on her tightened. The heels of his palms pressed into her hip bones, his fingers molding to the curve of her waist.

She tingled as though her body was waking from a long slumber with renewed circulation.

He growled, deepening the kiss, stroking her tongue

with lush, greedy slides of his own. All the oxygen was sucked from her lungs, and her thoughts evaporated in a stab of pure longing.

With her breasts crushed to his chest, his heart raged against her sternum, the beat guiding her own pulse. He pulled her hips forward, making her achingly aware of every hard, hot, aroused inch of him.

She'd never needed anything more than to have the solid pressure of his body against hers, his sinewy strength and leashed control wrapped around her.

His hips rubbed against her inner thighs, the friction creating a deeper ache that made her forget about the pain in her body. Awakened a yearning for something wild and passionate, caution and reason thrown to the wind.

Nick was the perfect man to give it to her.

A throat cleared in the doorway. They both jumped, pulling apart and looking embarrassed. But Nick stayed close, keeping one hand on her hip.

Renee stood on the threshold. "Excuse me. I'm sorry to interrupt, but I wanted you to know that I tried to call my mother."

"You did what?" Nick snapped, his face turning furious. "I explained how precarious this situation is. Her life is on the line."

"I meant well. Yes, you're the professional, but I knew if you spoke to Mom face-to-face for two minutes, you'd know without a doubt that you can trust her."

Nick's jaw clenched. "You shouldn't have gone behind my back and—"

Lori put her palm to his chest. "Nick, you were going to ask her to call the sheriff anyway."

He turned to Lori, his brow creased. "That's not the point."

"No, it's not," Renee said. "If you'd let me finish. I said I *tried* to call her. I couldn't get through. The phone line is down."

A fresh wave of tension sloshed in Lori's stomach. *Don't overreact. It doesn't mean anything.*

"Is that unusual for the phone to go on the fritz in this area?" he asked, taking out his cell.

"In a storm, sometimes it goes down. Otherwise, yes, it's unusual. And I couldn't get a signal on my cell."

Nick checked his phone. He looked up and shook his head. "No signal, either."

Her heart pounded hard as a fist against her sternum. The waking nightmare at the mall and the safe house resuscitated, engulfing her once more. The ache returned to Lori's throat on the next swallow, spreading with the next breath.

The apparatus the woman had used to try and strangle her was called a garrote. A word she wished she had never learned and now would never forget. Right along with the devastating force and heat of the explosion.

What new horror would be imprinted on her brain in the next few minutes?

"Do you have a two-way radio?" Nick asked.

Renee shook her head. "I don't."

A loud ding made Lori's pulse spike and she took a startled breath. "What is that?"

Nick went rigid. That internal switch in him had flipped and he was once again the icy, detached marshal prepared to annihilate anyone who sought to do her harm.

"Front doorbell," Renee said. "Someone's here."

Oh, God. Dr. Holmes had told them that she didn't have any appointments this afternoon. What if it was another assassin?

Would an assassin ring the bell?

No one can protect you. It's only a matter of time. A matter of when and how they kill you. But they will, if you agree to testify. Her father-in-law's words came back to her in an insidious rush. She tamped down the hot bile spurting up her throat.

Nick drew his gun.

"It's probably one of the deputies," Renee said. "He must have driven by, maybe tried phoning to see why I'm closed, couldn't reach me and decided to ring the bell."

Yeah, maybe that was it. Lori prayed that it was the sheriff's department outside, but her luck today had been BAD. Beyond Altogether Disastrous.

The odds weren't in her favor.

"Let's take a look," Nick said. "Is there any way to see who is out front without going into the reception area?"

The accordion-style security gate was designed to deter breaking and entering, but whoever was out front could clearly see the reception area and front desk.

"We have a security camera. We can access the live feed and intercom from my office."

"Perfect," Nick said.

Renee led the way. Nick tried to get Lori to stay in the exam room, but she wasn't having it. She slipped on her shoes and followed them to the office.

They huddled around the computer screen on the desk as Renee brought up the footage.

A middle-aged lady, maybe late fifties, early sixties,

stood outside holding a pet carrier with a dog inside. Behind her was an illegally parked black SUV with tinted windows. From the angle the car sat, it was impossible to tell if anyone else was inside.

"See what she wants and get rid of her," Nick said.

Renee hit a button for the intercom. "Can I help you?"

"Hello! Are you open? My dog is very sick. He's been throwing up all morning." She waved her free hand around as she spoke, gesturing wildly. "I'm worried he's dehydrated and might have worms or something. Can you check him out? It's an emergency." With her streamlined skirt and cute-as-a-button hat, the lady resembled an older Mary Poppins.

Relief ebbed through Lori, but Nick's eyes narrowed, his body coiled in readiness.

Renee looked to Nick.

"You can't open those doors," he said.

"But I have to. I'm obligated." Renee straightened in defiance. "There's a sick dog out there."

"Look," he said, taking on that hard-bitten, drill-sergeant tone that was worse than nails on a chalkboard. "I can't go into the details of what we've been through, but I'm telling you, not everyone is who they seem to be. You can't open those doors."

"Do you really think it's them?" Lori asked.

"Yes, it's them. It's no coincidence that the landline went dead and we lost cell service at the exact same moment that woman showed up."

Lori shook her head, not wanting to believe it, hoping there was another explanation. "How could they have found us here?"

"Damn Draper. It had to be him."

"Your boss?" Lori forced air into her lungs so her voice didn't sound so brittle. "You think he's a part of this?" Working for the cartel?

You have no idea who they own, who they've got in their back pocket working for them. Let this go. Otherwise it'll be your funeral. Her father-in-law had warned her, but she didn't listen.

"Excuse me!" the lady said. "Pepper already had one seizure today. Please, help us."

Renee put a palm to her stomach like the thought of turning away Mary Poppins and her little dog was too much to bear. "When I agreed to help you, I didn't sign on for turning away sick pets. The next vet is over thirty minutes away. I have to let her in."

"No, you don't," Nick said. "If she waited this long to bring that mutt in, she can drive thirty minutes. Renee, I'm asking you to trust me. Tell her to go to a different vet."

When Renee didn't appear persuaded to comply, Lori turned to her. "The people after me almost killed me three times today. Nick is the reason I'm not dead." She swallowed past the cold lump in her throat. "Please, listen to him."

Renee sighed, her gaze lowering like she was deliberating. Finally, she nodded and pressed the intercom. "I'm sorry, but we're closed because the computers are down. I hate to turn you away. Truly, I do, but there's another veterinary clinic not too far from here." Renee rattled off the address.

Nick stared at the monitor. They all waited to see how the lady would respond. Lori half expected the woman to pull out an Uzi and open fire.

The rear passenger's side door of the SUV opened. A brunette alighted from the car.

Lori's belly clenched. Was that the woman who'd been in the clothing store browsing earlier? Same chic bun, elegant movements, petite and pretty.

Oh, crap. It *was* her.

The brunette slammed the car door shut and approached the clinic in long, sure strides.

Queasiness took root in the pit of Lori's stomach.

"I knew it," Nick said. "Black Rose is behind this. It's another setup."

"Who?" Lori asked.

"That's what I've been calling her in my head from the tattoo on her hand. She's the puppet master pulling the strings of all the marionettes who've attacked you today."

Lori was too shocked to speak, her gaze glued to the monitor.

Black Rose walked straight up to the front door, looked up at the camera and waved.

Chapter Seven

Panic-stricken, Lori couldn't move. All the air whooshed from her lungs. A hundred different thoughts buzzed in her mind, but none fell from her lips.

On the monitor, Black Rose lifted her hand above her head and snapped her fingers. The lady holding the dog carrier did an about-face as a man hopped out of the SUV. He carried a briefcase, set flat atop both his hands, and walked up beside Black Rose.

"Dr. Holmes, do you mind if I call you Renee? So much more personal without the formality of titles. Don't you think?" Her tone was casual, freaking normal.

This couldn't be happening.

"Ask her name?" Nick said to Renee.

Renee pressed the intercom. "What do I call you?"

"Belladonna." A plastic grin tugged at her lips. She tapped the top of the briefcase next to her. The man opened it, revealing bundles of cash.

Renee and Lori gasped at the same time. Nick's hardened expression didn't waver, a flash of fury in his eyes. The heavy silence in the office seemed to press in on them.

"We can be friendly about this, Renee," Belladonna

said. "Unlock the door, pull up the gate and step aside. Simple. Step aside and take care of those beautiful, innocent creatures. In return, the briefcase and its contents are yours. All I want is the woman."

What if the FBI was wrong and the cartel was too big to be stopped? What if the US Marshals couldn't protect her? What if Draper was in on this? What if Nick—

No, no. Lori squashed such thoughts. Fear was poison. She couldn't let it pollute her mind. Testifying was the right thing to do. She wouldn't second-guess her decision.

There was no way to turn back the clock, unring that bell, anyway. Her course was set.

Lori had to trust Nick to get her through this alive and she clung to that like a lifeline.

Renee hit the intercom. "The sheriff is on the way. I've just phoned her. Any minute, deputies will be here. I suggest you leave."

Nick clicked his tongue, irritation stretched across his face. "Why would you say that?"

Renee shook her head, her eyes wide with fright, and shrugged. "To make them leave."

Nick huffed an audible breath in response.

"That's not true." Belladonna wagged a manicured finger at the camera and tsked. "Seeing as how I've cut your landline and blocked your cellular reception. This friendship isn't going to work if we lie to each other."

"What are we going to do?" Lori asked, struggling to filter panic from her voice and failing miserably.

"I'm going to be completely forthright with you, Renee," Belladonna said. "You owe the two individuals you're harboring absolutely nothing. You have one of two choices. I'm a fan of option number one, where you open the doors, take the money and turn a blind eye. Or there's option two." Belladonna winced. "I set this clinic on fire. Think of all those poor, defenseless dogs inside. I will fry each and every one of them right along with you. If that's what it will take to see the woman that I want dead." She raised her palms in the gesture of a minister delivering the gospel. "I'll give you a minute to talk amongst yourselves."

The room spun. Lori clutched the counter to keep from falling down. She hauled in a deep breath in an effort to calm the frenzied pounding of her heart.

"You can't open the doors," Nick said. "She'll kill you either way."

Renee pressed a fist to her mouth and turned away from him. "The two of you have to leave. I have to let her in. I can't jeopardize the animals in my care. I'm sorry."

"It's suicide." Lori stepped around in front of her. "Those people out there are heartless. Ruthless. You can't trust them."

"That's a chance I have to take. I swore an oath when I became a veterinarian and I meant it. I can't allow those animals to die. Not when I have the power to stop them from being burned alive by opening that door. If that means trading my life for theirs, then so be it." Renee rubbed her forehead. "I couldn't live with myself otherwise. Go. Go now. The back door leads to outdoor space for the dogs. It's surrounded by a six-foot cinder-block wall. Go over the right side. It's adjacent to the parking lot of the gas station."

"That's where our car is," Lori said. Nick had thought it best not to park in front of the clinic.

"Come with us," Nick said. "It's the only smart play. The three of us get out of here together."

"I think we both know that's not going to happen," Renee said. "If I can stop her from burning down my clinic, from killing…" The words seemed to back up in her throat as she looked out at all the caged animals. "I have to stay."

Nick nodded. "I did know you'd say that, but I had to try."

"I'll stall, buy you a few minutes. As long as I can," Renee said.

"Is there a back way we can take to the sheriff's to stay off the state road?"

Renee nodded. She scrawled directions on a notepad, tore it off and handed it to Nick. "Make it there and my mom, Sheila Holmes, will help you."

"Thank you, for helping us." Lori hugged her, hating that she'd not only endangered a kind veterinarian, but also defenseless animals. "I'm sorry we brought trouble to your door."

"I need your decision, Renee," Belladonna said. "I'm on a tight schedule and can't afford to wait any longer."

Renee pulled back from the embrace. "Go." She shooed them toward the back. "Hurry."

Nick grabbed the body armor, threw it on Lori, not taking the time to worry about concealing it, and led her to the exit.

Behind them, Lori heard Renee say, "Okay, okay! I don't want any of the animals hurt. Please."

"Excellent decision. I'm a dog lover, you know. Nothing against cats. But thank you for sparing me the moniker of The Pet Butcher. I mean, who wants to put that on their résumé?"

"No one, I suppose."

"Open up, Renee."

"I will. I swear. Let me grab my keys." Renee waved Nick and Lori out the back door.

They rushed through the noisy room that housed the dogs and cats, past the exam room, toward the exit. Lori glanced around for something she could use as a weapon. Anything could be waiting for them out back and she'd have to do her part to help Nick. To save herself.

She stopped in front of the fire extinguisher and hefted it off the wall. "I could swing it like a bat, clobber someone with it."

Nick pulled the safety pin from the extinguisher. "Better to spray someone in the face first."

Their gazes locked and something passed between them that didn't need words. A feeling, a jolt of understanding. They nodded to each other. No matter what, they'd get through this together.

They hurried to the back door.

"Do you think Belladonna will kill her?" Lori asked.

"Renee is as good as dead, but I think the animals have a fair shot at making it."

GUN UP AGAINST his chest, Nick was ready for anything. His heart beat a slow, steady cadence. Adrenaline pumped in his veins, sharpening his focus and reflexes. He turned the key, unlocking the dead bolt, and flung the door open.

Nick crossed the threshold. Sensed movement from the right side before he saw it.

He caught the gun hand of a big man that was taking aim, and the meathead did likewise, seizing Nick's wrist. A standoff where neither could shoot.

A second man closed in on Lori. She let the fire extinguisher rip, spraying him in the face with a blast of foamy chemicals.

The massive guy in front of Nick turned out to be as slow as he looked. Nick went for one of his knees with his boot heel.

No matter how big or how strong an opponent, take out his knees and he was done.

The connection of the steel boot shank and kneecap made a god-awful sound as the man howled in agony and dropped.

Nick kicked the gun from his hand and threw a powerful knee into the big guy's skull.

Whirling around, he snatched the fire extinguisher from Lori and throttled her attacker. Without a suppressor, discharging his gun would only broadcast their escape.

Once Lori's assailant stopped moving, he turned back to the other guy to finish the job. Nick kept swinging the extinguisher—hoisting it up overhead and slamming it down full force—until he was one hundred percent certain that neither man would ever get up again.

He scanned one hundred eighty degrees. All clear.

Nick beckoned to Lori. She took his hand as they crossed the long, narrow run of the grassy play area. It wasn't until then that he noticed the air reeked of feces and rain.

Fat, dark clouds had moved in and the sky looked on the brink of opening any minute. All they needed was a downpour on top of everything else. As if the progressively worsening situation wasn't bad enough.

Things kept getting worse and worse as Belladonna somehow stayed on their heels.

If he found out for certain that Draper was behind this, so help him God, there'd be payback. Nick would make it slow and painful, make Draper want to weep and beg for prison, but first he had to make sure that Lori was safe.

Survival was the focus now.

They scrambled to the east wall. Nick holstered his Glock and took a running leap. He snagged the top of the wall, hopped up and glanced over.

No more goons in sight.

Nick straddled the wall and proffered a hand to Lori. "Jump up."

She did and he caught her arm, then he reached for her other hand. She put her feet on the wall, and he pulled, helping her walk up the slab of cinder blocks.

They hopped down to the ground side by side and duckwalked to the parked vehicle.

Once Lori was inside, he said, "Stay low. I'll be right back and have you in my sights the entire time."

She didn't ask questions and trusted him. "Okay."

He closed the door quietly and looked around for any signs of approaching danger. There was nothing. Still, his guard was up, and he didn't dare entertain relief.

Nick slinked around to the far side of the gas station and peeked around the corner at the vet clinic.

The steel security gate was up. A second SUV was parked in front, and one armed guard stood watch.

Belladonna must've been inside.

For Renee's sake, he hoped he was wrong and that she'd make it through this ordeal alive.

"PLEASE, HAVE A SEAT, Renee," Belladonna said in a tone that was sweet without pouring it on so thick it sounded phony. Even if it was. One caught more flies with honey than vinegar, yada, yada, and all those other pearls of wisdom that were true.

Belladonna gestured to the chair in the back office.

Renee sat, trembling, her gaze darting to the hall where armed men were searching the place. Belladonna had no doubt that her quarry had already fled, and her men would find nothing in the clinic. After all, Mc-Kenna was a slippery bastard, but he didn't realize that even though they were on the move, the noose was tightening around Lori Carpenter's neck.

Belladonna pulled out a chair and sat opposite Renee, crossing her legs. They'd have a civilized conversation. Woman to woman.

If all went as expected, not a drop of blood would be shed.

"Are you going to kill me?" The vet's voice cracked as she swallowed a sob.

"You did as I asked and I'm a woman of my word." Belladonna folded her hands in her lap. "The briefcase is yours, as promised."

Renee's face twisted in disgust. "I don't want your blood money."

Belladonna chuckled. "Well then, we have a problem. I trust those who can be bribed to stay quiet. The self-righteous, who cling to their principles, not so much."

In the silence that followed, she let that sink in. Gave the vet a chance to see reason so they could come to a mutually satisfactory end.

Yes, Belladonna had been trained to be ruthless, to

kill without discrimination, or hesitation. But time had seasoned her, made her wiser.

A smart assassin lived longer than a brutal one. And sometimes showing mercy wasn't the same as leaving a loose end. She only had to be prudent enough to distinguish between the two.

"Consider the money a donation to your clinic," Belladonna said. "And reassurance that you'll have a faulty memory about today. About what you've seen. What you've heard. Who you've spoken to."

"Fine." Renee nodded.

Two rooks entered the room.

"They're not here," Smokey said.

As to be expected. Belladonna nodded once in acknowledgment.

"I'll call housekeeping." Max took out his phone.

The new rook was an eager beaver, but he was jumping the gun. Did he think she was bluffing about letting the woman live and not torching puppies and kittens?

That kind of thing didn't even go over well in prison. Those who hurt children and animals had a tough go behind bars. Not that Belladonna was going to see the inside of a jail cell.

She raised her hand, stopping him from making the call.

Renee's chin lifted. "As you can see, they're not here. Please, I'm begging you to leave. I won't say a word to anyone."

"First, I have some questions."

Renee shook her head. "I don't know anything."

"That's not entirely true, is it?" Belladonna asked. "Where are they going?"

"Follow them and you'll find out." Renee shifted in her seat, gaze darting to the phone on the desk.

The line was back up and in working order. Little did Renee realize. Not that she would've gotten the chance to dial 911.

"Believe me, they are being followed." Once Belladonna had pinpointed their location to the veterinary clinic, she'd posted men at either end of the state road to intercept them in case McKenna and the woman managed to get out.

Then there was the fact that she was tracking McKenna's electronic fingerprint and eavesdropping on all his cellular calls. As long as she prevented them from meeting up with those SOG operators, Belladonna had this in the bag.

"But I want to know their intended destination," Belladonna said, "and whether or not the men I have in position will be able to cut them off before they get there."

"I don't know where they're going. The second you showed up, they hightailed it out of here."

That was almost believable. *Almost.* "I'm a patient woman. Truly, I am." Sometimes Belladonna had to lie in wait for hours, days, for the opportune moment to strike a target. She had patience in spades. "But I'm short on time. I should mention that I have a keen sense of smell. I can detect BS from a mile out. So imagine how strong the stench is when you're sitting two feet away. Where are they going?"

Renee pursed her lips and gripped the edge of her chair.

The doctor knew exactly where they were headed.

"Friends cooperate. And I want us to remain friends," Belladonna said, annoyance leaking into her voice.

Renee seemed to make a split-second decision and opened her mouth.

Belladonna sensed the fib forming on her tongue and stopped her. "Before you answer, understand that I will view a lie as cause to renegotiate our agreement. This *conversation* will turn into an *interrogation* and I'll be forced to introduce you to a level of pain you've never known. In the end, your life will be forfeit. Take a second to process that. Now, where are they going?"

Renee whimpered. "The sheriff's department. But there's no point in going there. You can't bribe or intimidate the sheriff. And it's not like you can have a shoot-out in the middle of the town. The State Police are only thirty minutes away and they'll respond to any report of hostile action."

Hmm. Renee was well informed. But it would only take the State Police ten minutes to pop up due to an inopportune three-car pile-up close by on State Route 18. Four squad cars were already on the scene.

Belladonna didn't have the luxury of engaging in a lengthy shoot-out with McKenna and the sheriff's department hunkered down to protect Carpenter.

Any action she took had to either be quiet or quick.

"I bet you thought you were above bribery and intimidation, too, until you weren't," Belladonna said.

"The sheriff is different. My mother won't negotiate with terrorists. Or whatever the hell you are. So you might as well give this up and leave that poor woman alone."

Mother? The plot thickened to the sublime consistency of pudding. "If only it were that simple." Belladonna licked her lips and leaned forward, resting her forearms on her thighs. "The marshal and the woman.

Did there appear to be anything amorous between them?"

"What?" Renee stiffened in her chair.

McKenna had to have a weakness. Belladonna bet it was Lori Carpenter. Both of them were healthy, young, attractive, single, heterosexual, and they'd been in close quarters every day for a year.

"Oh, you don't understand the question?" Belladonna snapped her fingers and Smokey left the room.

Nothing more was required. Not a single word needed to be uttered. Her longtime rooks and bishops knew how she operated well enough to intuit what she wanted with the snap of her fingers or the lift of a palm. Smokey was practically her right hand. She was training Max, which was hard to do on the fly.

A moment later Smokey returned, holding a dog in his arms. An adorable poodle. Hypoallergenic, nonshedding; her daughter would love one exactly like it.

Smokey scratched the pooch's head and showered it with adoration.

Renee reared back with a hand flying to her collarbone. Tears welled in her eyes. "Don't. You can't. Please."

"Let's try again," Belladonna said, knowing the threat was sufficient, and that no animals would be harmed during this intimidation tactic. "Did they appear to be intimate, show any signs that their relationship was more than professional?"

"Yes, yes. I walked in on them kissing."

Interesting. Belladonna had expected to hear details of a hug, a comforting look that had lingered too long, the two of them holding hands. Kissing was better. Concrete.

"Please, don't hurt Bailey," Renee said, sniffling.

Belladonna gave a nod, and Smokey handed the dog off to someone in the hall to return to its cage.

"Thank you." Renee sobbed, looking overwrought from the conversation.

That one had a delicate constitution.

"No. Thank *you*," Belladonna said, standing up. The doctor had turned out to be a gold mine of information and would prove even more useful.

Max raised his gun and aimed it at the doctor.

Belladonna knocked his arm down. "What are you doing?"

"The boss doesn't want any witnesses," Max said.

Oh, hell no, those words didn't just leave his mouth.

A cold anger chilled her heated blood. "I need her, you idiot." She slapped him hard, backhanded, to remind not only him, but also all her people, of their place. "Who is running this mission?"

"You," he said through clenched teeth.

Dante Vargas, the west coast cartel cell leader, was technically in charge and was Belladonna's boss. But she called the tactical shots in the field.

"Who is in charge, right here?" she asked.

Max rubbed his red cheek and glared at her, murderous intent gleaming in his eyes.

Fury speared through her at having to ask twice. "Who?"

"You."

"Too bad you forgot that." Now she had to make him an example.

Leniency in this situation only invited insubordination. Perhaps even mutiny, where someone might stab her in the back, thinking they'd finish the job themselves, outshine her and earn a promotion.

Like she didn't have enough to worry about without that crap, too. She nodded to Smokey. He swept up behind Max, quicker than a blink, and slipped a garrote around his throat.

It took a lot longer than a slug to the brainpan to kill someone this way, but it was quieter and less mess.

Renee let out a horrified squeak, jumping out of her chair, and scurried back into a corner.

Good instincts.

Belladonna shifted out of the range of the struggle that ensued—not wanting to catch a stray kick from Max's steel-toed boots.

Drawing a fortifying breath, she took out her cell and made the call. "I need cleanup."

Another rook stepped into the office and grabbed Max's feet to help. The two of them wrangled Max's body taut and a gurgle came from him as he clutched his throat.

Belladonna smiled, her fury thinning to oblivion. *Teamwork makes the dream work.*

"Veterinary?" the female voice said over the phone.

"Yes." Belladonna ran a hand over her hair, ensuring not a single strand had been knocked loose. "One body."

"On it."

Smokey removed the wire from around Max's throat. The two rooks let the lifeless body hit the floor in a heap.

Crisis averted. Good thing she nipped that in the bud.

Belladonna turned to her rooks. "One of you, help the doctor into my trunk."

"B-b-but, you said you'd let me live." Renee squeezed into the corner as though trying to disappear into the wall.

"I'm afraid your life is no longer in my hands," Belladonna said, putting her cell away. "Whether you live or die today will be up to your mother. The sheriff."

Chapter Eight

Maybe going to the sheriff's department wasn't a good idea. Everything Nick touched turned to blood.

The thought of endangering more people kicked up a thrumming in his temples.

But that was the point of law enforcement; they weren't ordinary civilians like Dr. Renee Holmes, and the sheriff was the closest. Though he had a niggling suspicion that this situation exceeded the capabilities of the local sheriff, whose biggest problem was probably some meth heads pulling a little B and E in the area.

With Belladonna hot on their heels, and his SOG teammates hours away, the fact that they needed assistance was a dire understatement.

"Are you sure we should still go to the sheriff?" Lori asked as though reading his mind.

The only thing he was certain of was that he had to do everything in his power to keep her alive. "I was wondering the same thing. I don't think we have much choice."

If he kept Draper out of the loop and updated Yazzie directly about their new location, Belladonna shouldn't be able to find them. There was no reason for Belladonna to think that the vet had any clue of their intentions and unfortunately, Renee had probably caught a bullet to the frontal lobe two seconds after she opened the door.

He drove down the dirt path Renee had told them to take in order to stay off main streets and looked for the fork in the road, where they needed to turn.

"Will her mother still help us once she learns we abandoned her daughter, left her to the mercy of assassins?"

"We didn't *abandon* her. Though we did leave her. Belladonna had threatened to burn down the clinic if Renee didn't open the doors. The doctor was hellbent on ensuring those animals were safe." Not that he blamed her for following her conscience. Even if it was a reckless decision.

"That may be," Lori said, "but it doesn't feel like we made the right choice. I know we couldn't have fought them off there, but I hate to think about what might have happened to Renee. She was only being a good person, trying to help us."

There went Lori's big heart again, worrying more about others than herself. "We made the only choice we could." He reached over and took her hand.

Her thin, cold fingers closed around his, and the tension in her eased a bit. She rested her head on his shoulder. He pressed his lips to her soft hair.

Knowing how to console a witness and assuage their worries was part of the job, but this was different. Seeing the wave of fear recede from her at his touch filled him with an indescribable warmth.

He didn't date much. His job kept him so damn busy that it was part of the reason he'd hooked up with Charlie in the first place. She was attractive and it had been convenient for them both, but that train had never left the casual station. He'd had absolutely no affect on her. She'd treated him like a sexual Lego block.

With Lori, there was a bond he couldn't explain. Maybe it was a result of the time they'd spent together, with him not only attending to all her needs from groceries, to seeing a dentist, to reassurance about the trial, but also caring about her.

Somewhere along the way, he'd grown to need her, too.

His first thought in the morning and his last in the evening were of her. The most beautiful thing in the world was Lori's smile. He had vivid dreams about her and even more erotic fantasies of her writhing in pleasure beneath him, but what he craved was this closeness.

They hit another bump, jostling the car. He slowed from fifty to forty, working their way from one end of town to the other. The scenic route took longer, but it was smarter to stay off the main thoroughfare. Belladonna might have lookouts posted, waiting to ambush them.

The only problem was this road was narrow and unpaved. If another car came from the opposite direction, he had no idea what he was supposed to do. It wasn't as if there was enough room to pull over. It was a mystery how the locals managed.

One thing about this back road—it was quiet and removed from the touristy energy of town. It almost made it possible to push from the forefront of his mind that evil wasn't far behind, circling, poised to strike, to kill the beautiful, warm woman at his side.

That was precisely why he didn't shove the knowledge away and kept it front and center instead. Belladonna was cunning and sharp as a switchblade. If he let his guard slip, gave that assassin one inch, she'd take a yard and hang Lori with it.

He had to stay vigilant and on point. A single mistake could cost them both their lives.

"You didn't answer my question," she said, sitting up and looking at him. "Do you think the sheriff will help us?"

"Her mother sounds like a Dudley Do-Right. Duty first. If that's the case, she'll feel just as obligated to help us and to protect you as Renee did about the animals."

"I hope so." She gave him a weak smile.

The fork in the road was up ahead. Once they turned, it was less than a ten-minute ride to the sheriff's dept. He gave her fingers a comforting squeeze and put both hands on the wheel.

His cell phone buzzed in his pocket.

Damn it. He should've gotten rid of it before they started their backwoods trek to the sheriff's department.

Nick fished the cell out from his jacket pocket and read the caller ID on the screen. "Draper." He cursed under his breath, weighing how to respond. Not thirty minutes after the last time they'd spoken, Belladonna had located them and made her move.

Experience, his gut—hell, common sense—told him it wasn't coincidence.

Draper didn't have to call Nick to track his phone, but he was going through the trouble of phoning for a reason. What did he want? What new angle was he going to play?

Nick answered. "McKenna."

"The working group I put together from Intel and

IT to figure out how we've been breached finally came up with an answer," Draper said, excitement buzzing in his voice.

Now, that was unexpected and certainly worth taking the call, but could Nick trust anything Draper said?

He hit the speaker icon, letting Lori hear firsthand whatever explanation Draper was going to try to sell him. "Really. What did they find?"

"You're not going to believe this," Draper said, and Nick silently agreed that he probably wouldn't. "Our system has been hacked."

Talk about throwing him for a loop. Then again, it was the punch you didn't see coming that knocked you out.

He glanced at Lori. The mix of curiosity and wariness stamped on her face reflected how Nick felt but refused to show.

"Hacked?" Nick asked. "How? Are they sure?"

"They're certain someone has been fishing around in our system, but they haven't figured out how yet. No firewalls were breached. Whoever hacked us is smart, masking their point of entry, not staying too long at any given sweep, dipping in and out of the system, extracting data."

This was a digital world. Every report on Hummingbird was electronic, logged in the database. A breach of their system gave a plausible explanation for how Belladonna would've known in advance that they would be at the mall. What time. Which store. Even the entrance and exit they had planned to use had all been spelled out in the reports. Also, when deputies were out in the field on high-priority missions like this one, their cell's geolocator could be retrieved with a few keystrokes.

Anyone with access could've tracked him to the veterinary clinic.

All of it was plausible. And convenient.

"Do they know how long we've been compromised?" Nick asked, dreading the answer. Hours, days, weeks, a month?

Jeez. The amount of sensitive, confidential information that could've been stolen was bone-chilling.

Long-term, this might impact more than Lori.

"They have no idea how long we've been exposed yet," Draper said. "They just discovered it. But once they have an opportunity, they're going to go over everything with a fine-tooth comb."

The USMS employed some of the best techies in the business. With such high stakes, they would run this to ground and ascertain their level of exposure. Hopefully, sooner rather than later.

"You said that our firewall wasn't hacked," Nick said.

"Right."

"Doesn't that mean whoever has been extracting data had internal access?"

Lori paled at his question.

Draper heaved a sigh into the phone. "Unfortunately, yes, it does."

"Is the person still in the system?"

"IT has closed all network nodes accessible from outside the building. We've enacted limited restricted access within the building. If the breach emanated from a computer in this building, IT will find it. I've instated a temporary lockdown. No one in or out until each CPU has been checked. But don't worry. Yazzie and Killinger are en route."

Nick could practically hear Draper's wheels spinning

through the phone. The challenges had been identified and his boss was working viable solutions, but only half the problem was being addressed.

"What if it wasn't a computer inside the building that was used to breach us?" Nick asked.

Draper had access to the system from his home. It enabled him to work late, on weekends and to respond to any situation at a moment's notice.

"Then we may never know who breached us or exactly what data they stole." Draper's voice was solemn. "The good news is they no longer have access."

Good, yeah, but once again, convenient. For Draper.

His boss had a trailblazing record, utterly spotless. Other districts referred to him as Mr. Clean. No matter what trouble or scandal befell an office, Draper saved his own skin and always walked away without a speck on him.

Either Draper was just good at playing the political game and climbing the ladder, or he was as dirty as they came.

"No outside nodes will be reopened until Hummingbird has testified, the network has been scrubbed and patches installed to prevent this from happening again," Draper said, giving a textbook answer.

"Sounds like you've got your hands full, juggling lots of balls in the air," Nick said. "The blowback from this breach could be catastrophic."

"Yeah, well, heavy is the head that wears the crown. My problem and not yours. You worry about keeping Hummingbird alive."

"That's getting tough to do with assassins popping up at every turn."

"Don't tell me you've had more trouble," Draper said,

almost sounding legitimately surprised and rather concerned.

Nick met Lori's weary eyes before looking back at the road. "As a matter of fact, we have. Assassins found us at the veterinary clinic."

Draper swore. "Hummingbird is okay, right? You're both okay?"

"Yes. We are. But sir, I have to go dark until I've made contact with Yaz and Killinger. I'll find an alternate location for the meet and notify them at the last minute."

"Hold on, McKenna. Don't be rash. If you're worried about your calls still being traced, get a burner phone."

"No. No more phone calls. No more updates."

"If you go *dark* and something happens to Hummingbird, after I'm done hanging your butt out to dry, you're fired."

Nick's blood pressure spiked at the threat. "And if I find out that you're dirty and had anything to do with our breach, you're dead."

He ended the call and stopped the car. Removing the battery from the phone, he got out of the vehicle. He dropped the cell and the battery on the ground and stomped both to pieces.

"We've got to pick up a burner," he said, climbing back in, and sped down the road. "I hope they sell flip phones in this small town."

"Why does it have to be an old-school flip phone?"

"Can't be traced."

"Could Draper be responsible for this?"

If Will Draper, the head of the San Diego office, was the source of their breach, it complicated the situation. For starters, Draper had his fingers in everything related to this mission and had both the district attorney and the US attorney's office on speed dial since the case involved state and federal crimes.

Nick would need irrefutable evidence to get anyone to take the accusation seriously. "I hope not."

"But you really think it's possible your boss is the one who has been feeding information to the drug cartel?"

Nick's scalp prickled. He was aware that the financial firm Lori had worked for, Wallace Capital Management, had been laundering money for dangerous people. Not knowing who WCM's clients were, he'd assumed the mob or some other organized crime group. "Which cartel?"

"Los Chacales."

The Jackals.

His gaze snapped to her. "Is that who Belladonna works for? Is that WCM's biggest client?" The world's most powerful and violent drug cartel?

"Yes."

Holy hell.

The deputies assigned to safeguard a witness before a trial weren't privy to all the details of the case outside what was covered in the news and what was considered essential need-to-know particulars. And Lori wasn't supposed to discuss the case.

Now he understood how US Attorney Foy was going to leverage this into a platform to run for governor. Drug cartels, especially ones as powerful and brutal as *Los Chacales*, were considered the largest growing threat to national security.

A win against WCM would also be lauded as a

win against the cartel. Talk about putting a feather in Foy's cap.

"How much of the cartel's money is being laundered through WCM?" he wondered aloud.

"Close to seventy-five percent."

Damn. This was insane.

The US attorney's office should've told the Marshals Service that Lori was going to be the biggest target in WITSEC in a decade. Hell, maybe ever.

What if they had informed Draper and that was the reason he had her squirreled away to a remote location three hours from San Diego, where there was zero chance of her being recognized?

But then somehow the cartel had gotten to him. Found out something about him they could use to coerce him, like gambling debts or deviant behavior?

Maybe it was as simple as greed, and they'd offered him more money than he could turn down.

With the breach of their database, anything could've been stolen, including the names, new identities and current addresses of all the people in the WITSEC program in the state of California. Not to mention the names and family members of every single deputy marshal and US Marshal in charge of a district office.

Forget about exploiting a person's financial troubles or hanging deviant behavior over their head. Snatch someone's kid and then ask that deputy or marshal what they were willing to do to keep their child alive.

Nick bet the answer would be *anything*.

Draper shared custody of his high-school-age son with his ex-wife. It wouldn't have been difficult for a skilled assassin to reach out and touch them.

The cartel would go to extraordinary lengths to stop Lori from testifying if it was going to hem up seventy-five percent of their money-laundering operation.

Seventy-five. "How do you know WCM was cleaning seventy-five percent of the cartel's money?"

Her eyes shifted away a second. "I was the accountant assigned to that client's portfolio."

That gave her access to everything the cartel would've invested, but something about Lori's explanation didn't jibe. "Yeah, okay, but you would only know how much WCM cleaned for them and how much was the firm's cut. Not what percentage that was of the cartel's entire bankroll."

Unless she had information from inside the cartel itself.

If he hadn't lifted his gaze from the road to glance at her, he might have missed it. Hell, even though he'd seen it, that flash of alarm in her eyes had popped up and vanished so quickly, he doubted his eyesight.

"What are you suggesting?" she asked, reeling away against the passenger door. "Are you accusing me of something?"

"I'm not accusing you of anything. I'm trying to understand because this isn't adding up."

"I don't know what you want me to say."

"How about the truth." He didn't think she was lying per se, but she wasn't being completely forthright. She was hiding something from him. The question was, what?

He was aware she had an immunity deal, but he'd assumed it was to protect her if she had unwittingly done something that she could be charged for later. Now he wasn't so sure.

"Why do you have an immunity clause in your deal to testify?"

She narrowed her eyes, lifting the wall between them. "Aren't the specifics of a witness's deal supposed to be confidential? Not even deputy marshals are supposed to know, right?"

Whoa. Her throwing in his face that she was a witness and he was a deputy hurt worse than a kick to the gut. She was correct and entirely justified if she felt he'd violated her privacy. But the sting of her words told him that he'd lost professional objectivity.

"Yes, it's supposed to be confidential." Nick only knew because he'd overheard Draper at the tail end of a conversation with the US attorney's office. "But answering a question with a question isn't really giving me an answer."

Lori shook her head, withdrawing into herself. "I went to the FBI when I didn't have to. I was doing my civic duty, trying to do the right thing. This is a job for you, but it's *my* life that's being ripped to shreds. Those assassins are hunting *me*. So why do I feel like I'm the one on trial here?"

Forget a kick to the gut; this was a boot heel to the teeth. "I didn't mean for you to take it like that."

"I took it the way you intended, and don't use that tone with me."

"What tone?"

"Oh, please." She waved a hand at him in disgust. "As if you don't know. It's one thing to use it while barking out orders to protect me. It's another thing to unleash it to intimidate me."

He smothered the frustration simmering inside. Snapping at her wasn't going to achieve anything.

"Look," he said, making his tone Charmin-soft, "knowing exactly what we're dealing with will help me protect you."

"I found out WCM was laundering money for *Los Chacales* and went to the FBI. The cartel put a price on my head. Now Belladonna and her merry band of killers are gunning for me. End of story. What more do you need to know to keep me alive?"

He was on her side. The only thing standing between her and a hot slug to the back of the head. Yes, she was an assignment and he was professionally obligated to protect her, but he meant it when he'd told her that he'd rather cut off his right arm than hurt her. He sure as hell would jump in the line of fire and take a bullet for her and that didn't have a damn thing to do with his job.

If she didn't have anything to hide, then she wouldn't be so defensive. Evasive. Throwing out the reminder of her confidentiality clause like a yellow flag on a football play.

"I get that this is personal for your in-laws." He did his best to bottle his rising anger. "But I need to know if this is also personal for the cartel?"

Lori folded her arms across her chest and straightened. She wasn't budging.

"Hundreds of millions of dollars are at stake," she said. "I don't think it gets more personal than that. Do you?"

She did it again. Used a whole lot of words to avoid giving him a straight answer.

He pulled into a spot in front of a mobile phone store down the block from the sheriff's department and threw the gear into Park. As much as he wanted to continue this discussion, she didn't give him the chance.

Lori jumped out of the car and slammed the door.

Chapter Nine

Fuming, Lori stood on the sidewalk.

How had the conversation in the car spun so far out of control, so freaking fast? She'd let one little thing slip, and Nick picked it up and ran with it like a contestant on *The Amazing Race*.

That stubborn, willful, *gorgeous* man.

She was overwhelmed and scared and didn't need him ambushing her, too. Not when she was trying to catch her breath and make it through this the best way she knew how.

Nick shut his door and stalked over to her. "We can table the conversation for now, but don't think it's over," he said, irrepressible as always.

She rolled her eyes. "Of course not. Your ego couldn't handle that."

Incredulity eclipsed the banked indignation on his face. "My ego?"

"Yup. Because you weren't the one to decide *end of conversation.* You're like a dog with a bone, digging around in my business. My life." *Trying to unearth my secrets*. They were hers for one more day and then all her dirty laundry would be aired. "You and I both know full well that you don't need any of the answers to your questions to protect me."

He huffed at that. "You're right. I don't need the answers to do my job. But I do need them for my peace of mind."

Lori's brain was spinning to keep up with Nick's words. "What are you talking about?"

"To hell with the trial and the Marshals Service for a second. This—" he gestured between them "—is the first time I've had that *I give a damn* feeling for someone." His voice lowered, resonating with a gravelly heat that turned her center molten. "Yes, it's ill-timed and inappropriate, but if that bothered you, then you wouldn't have kissed me back. And woman, you kissed the hell out of me."

He pulled her into his arms, and she was tempted to run her fingers through his thick hair and absorb the security of his embrace, to yield to him in every way. But she couldn't.

"What I'm saying is, I'm crazy about you, Lori."

He wrapped an arm around her waist and caught her chin, forcing her to look at him. His thumb feathered across her cheek.

Heart racing, she gaped at him, overcome by his words and the uncharacteristic emotion that shone on his face.

"I know you like to dunk your peanut butter sandwiches in milk," he said. "That you won't eat Chinese food without chopsticks. That you hate carnations because they remind you of your mother's funeral. That charity work uplifts you, renews your spirit. It's your way of giving back since it was the Helping Hands

Foundation that saved you during those rough years with your dad."

This was killing her. She pressed her trembling fingertips to his lips to silence him. If he didn't stop, he was going to turn her into a mess. A big, sappy mess.

But he kissed the pads of her fingers and kept talking. "Your favorite book is *Wuthering Heights* and Heathcliff ruined you for life. Now you're only attracted to the dark, brooding, dangerous type. Lucky for me." He stared down at her, his smile sexy and devastating.

Deep in the pit of her stomach, she knew that no other man would look at her as he did right then. She wanted to burn this moment into her memory so she would never, ever forget it.

"But I have to know what I'm dealing with, who you are," Nick said. "All the cards on the table. It's the only way we can tell if this is real."

For a long, breathless moment, she was too choked up to speak. He wanted to see her layers, nothing more than she'd asked of him, but voicing the truth would snip this connection between them. Like cutting a tether. She couldn't bear that on top of everything else going on.

She couldn't breathe past the knot in her throat, but she forced herself to swallow down the ache. To ignore the hot flutter of desire.

"What difference does it make?" Desperation flooded her. "If I survive, after I testify, I'm gone and it's over, anyway."

Why put themselves through unnecessary heartache?

Better to leave well enough alone. She wrenched free of his grasp, hating the way she had been softening in his arms, and stormed into the cell-phone store. Spotting a small display of flip phones, she hurried to the rack.

Nick went up to her, drawing her attention like a tractor beam. "It matters to me. And I hope like hell that it matters to you, too."

Of course it mattered. No man had ever been so honest with her, shown her so much respect by opening up the way Nick had back at the clinic. It couldn't have been easy, and she admired his courage. The trust he'd shown her was a gift and a miracle rolled into one.

She understood what it meant. What it was worth.

Her reluctance to do the same made her the biggest hypocrite.

For someone who detested double standards, her omission sickened her, but she didn't have the strength for the cold slap of rejection that she'd face from him.

"There's no point," she said. "Please, drop it."

He nodded, his eyes growing cold. "Well, that's the most disappointing response I've ever heard." His tone was hard enough to crush a diamond, reminding her with blinding clarity that there was nothing soft about this man.

Not his body, or his mind, or his personality.

"Welcome back, Deputy Marshal Dredd. Did you have a nice ten-minute vacation?"

Regret stung her tongue. She wanted to hit Rewind and take those ugly words back. The man just told her he was crazy about her for goodness' sake, and instead of being honest, she pulled the rejection rip cord first and parachuted out.

"Wish I could say it was nice to see you, Lori 'The Chicken' Carpenter, but I'm not a liar. I had a fantastic vacation with an incredible woman until she lost her suitcase full of courage. Too bad she's not here now." He grabbed a phone and went to pay for it.

What in the hell could she say to that?

He was right. She was a coward.

Even more surprising, through the anger and the argument, the sexual tension arcing between them was a live wire crackling with heat.

She went up to the register where Nick was paying. The clerk cut the plastic packaging open for them and tossed it in the trash. Nick pocketed the phone.

They walked to the sheriff's department in silence. He opened the door for her, and she entered the vestibule on rubbery legs. She found she couldn't look at Nick. Not that he had done anything wrong. She'd probably have a harder time looking in the mirror.

He held the inner door for her, as well, and they approached the front desk.

"Hi, how can I help?" the twentysomething receptionist asked.

"I'd like to speak with Sheriff Sheila Holmes." He flashed his badge to the receptionist.

Lori glanced past the four empty desks spread out behind the receptionist to the sheriff's office. Through the office window, Lori spotted the sheriff engrossed in a lively conversation with a man about ten years her junior who was holding a pie.

The physical similarities between the sheriff and the vet were plain. The same slender build, olive complexion, friendly, heart-shaped face, mahogany hair—the sheriff's was pulled into a loose French braid.

"Certainly. One moment," the receptionist said.

Apparently, the office was so small and informal, she just spun around in her seat and beckoned the sheriff over with a hand.

Sheriff Holmes clasped the man on the arm and said

something to him that caused him to nod and hand her the pie.

She took it and walked him to the front. "Thanks again, Gerald, but if you keep bringing me these delicious pies, I'm not going to be able to fit into my uniform."

A tantalizing aroma curled around Lori and she realized that it had been more than six hours since she'd eaten.

"I've got to win you over some way, Sheila. I figured my best bet is through my baking. So, I'm not going to stop until you agree to have dinner with me. I've got a huckleberry recipe that'll knock your socks off." He winked.

The sheriff chuckled at that, the bright smile emphasizing the fine lines around her eyes and mouth. Then she caught sight of the bulletproof vest Lori was wearing and her laughter died.

"You better say yes," the receptionist said, still giggling, "before one of us gains fifteen pounds from eating all that sugary goodness."

"Thanks again." The sheriff's tone flattened as she gestured to the pie.

Gerald took the hint. He slipped on his ball cap, tipped the bill to her and was gone.

"Hello, I'm Sheriff Holmes." She set the pie on the counter and proffered her hand.

"Deputy Marshal Nick McKenna." He shook her hand. "Do you mind if we speak privately in your office?"

Up close, Lori noticed the same smattering of freckles across Sheila's nose that Renee had. They were both approachable and welcoming, but where Renee had been sweet, there was a discernible toughness to the sheriff.

"Not at all. Can we get you two anything?" the sheriff asked. "Water, coffee, strawberry-rhubarb pie?"

Lori's stomach answered with a loud rumble. "All three for me, please."

"I'll just have a water," Nick said.

The receptionist nodded. "I'll bring it in a moment."

"Thank you, Suzie," the sheriff said, and then led them to her office.

She invited them to sit in chairs opposite her desk and closed the door.

Once the sheriff was seated behind her desk, Nick said, "Ma'am, what I'm about to tell you is extremely sensitive and confidential. I'd appreciate your discretion."

"Okay." She folded her hands on the top of her desk. "I'm listening."

"This is Lori Carpenter. She's been in WITSEC for a year and is supposed to testify in an important trial tomorrow down in San Diego. My office has been compromised and her whereabouts leaked to *Los Chacales*. The drug cartel."

The sheriff's face hardened as she took everything in. "I'm familiar with them. A pretty dangerous group."

Dangerous? That was like calling a hurricane gale a breeze.

They seemed unstoppable and relentless. If the sheriff didn't help them, if this plan didn't work, Lori had no clue what they were going to do.

"Yes, ma'am. They are," Nick said.

The receptionist knocked and entered. She set a tray

down on the desk, passed around beverages, handed Lori a piece of pie and a fork.

The sheriff thanked Suzie again, and the receptionist left.

Lori dug in, scarfing down the slice of heaven in five bites before Nick got to the grisly parts and she lost her appetite. The sheriff studied her intently, gaze bouncing back to Nick every few seconds as he continued to explain.

"Four attempts have been made on her life since this morning, including at our safe house, which was rigged with explosives and killed my partner."

The sheriff's eyes narrowed, and she straightened. "The explosion on Mill Creek. That was you?"

Nick and Lori both nodded.

"Two of my deputies are out there now. The fire department recovered a body. I take it that was your partner," Sheriff Holmes said. "I'm sorry for your loss."

Nick hung his head. Guilt over Ted must've been heavy as sandbags on his shoulders by the looks of him.

"We barely survived," Lori said. "If it hadn't been for Nick, I wouldn't have. I owe him my life." She turned to him, but he refused to meet her eyes.

Lori owed him much more than that. A debt that couldn't be repaid.

At the very least, if they made it to the courthouse, she'd tell him how much he meant to her before they parted ways forever. Tell him that she was beyond crazy for him, totally over the moon and lost. Hopelessly lost in the sense of comfort and security his touch brought; lost in his incredible magnetism when they were in the same room; lost in his dark eyes when he looked at her.

And if she stared into them now, she'd drown in the bourbon-brown depths.

She ached at the thought of never jogging together again, no more long conversations, not playing board games, not watching movies, not cooking together and taste-testing recipes.

He'd given her so much, shown consideration for things in ways that Ted hadn't. Still, it might've just been him fulfilling his job duties, but the time they'd spent together had shown her how much she'd tolerated from others, how little she'd expected for herself and thought she deserved.

Although she was seated, she felt off balance. Her heart was breaking. The world was unraveling. She was going to lose her best friend.

Lori had had a handful of lovers and been married once, but none of those men had been her best friend. Or knew her as well as Nick did.

She couldn't hold back the tears welling in her eyes.

"Here." Sheriff Holmes handed her a box of tissues. "I'm sure today has been quite an ordeal for you."

"Yes, it has," Lori breathed.

Nick placed his hand on her shoulder and gave her a long sideways glance, the affection in his eyes saying he was there for her. The silent gesture was all he could do in front of someone else.

"Sheriff," he said, drawing his hand into his lap, "the cartel is still here. Close by."

Lori and Nick exchanged a look. She held her breath, waiting to see if he was going to mention Renee and what happened at the clinic.

"Special Operation Group deputies are coming up from San Diego to provide assistance," he said. "We need a safe place to wait and to keep Lori's name out of your system until then."

"Why hasn't the LA Marshals' office been notified?" the sheriff asked. "They're closer."

"I'm not a hundred percent sure. My boss, Will Draper, made the decision. Possibly to limit their involvement since we don't know if the leak could've come from their office. But ma'am, I have reason to believe that Marshal Draper might in fact be the breach."

Sheriff Holmes pursed her lips and leaned back in her chair, the leather groaning with the movement. "That's a pretty heavy accusation. Do you have anything to substantiate it?"

"No, ma'am. I'm afraid I don't."

Lori chugged a little water and then traded it for black coffee, bypassing the cream.

"Is there anyone who can corroborate your story?" Holmes asked.

"The marshals on their way up here can."

"Give me a number." She picked up the phone and waited.

"I'd prefer to hold off on notifying them until they're closer to the area," Nick said.

The silence that followed was tense.

Sheriff Holmes studied him a moment, looked to Lori, then back to him. "Why is that exactly?"

"As I've told you, we've been compromised," Nick said. "I think it might be my boss. He is the only person who has been aware of Lori's location up to thirty minutes ago, where the cartel last found us. But as you pointed out, I don't have proof. Therefore, I could be wrong. If we wait until my teammates are closer to Big

Bear Lake, then we've risked nothing. Tipping our hand sooner opens the door to the possibility of sabotage."

Holmes drew in a deep breath, seeming to weigh her options. The whole back-and-forth process agitated Lori's nerves.

"How about I ask the State Police to send a few squad cars over? Precautionary measure," the sheriff said.

"Would that request entail notifying them that a deputy marshal is in your office along with a star witness?" Nick asked.

"It would. To tap their resources requires a darn good reason. You have one, but to get them here means I have to share that reason."

"Then that's not a course of action I can endorse. No one can know we're here. The moment you make a call, it could be intercepted."

"I want to help, but you're not giving me much to work with while asking me to have a bucketful of faith in your story." She folded her arms. "What was the last location where you were attacked?"

Nick's gaze fell, but apart from that, Lori wanted to shake whatever he was thinking loose from his lips.

She didn't want to spoil any strategy he had planned, but Renee's situation, the predicament they had left her in, was eating Lori up inside. She couldn't stand it any longer and opened her mouth to confess what had happened.

"Sheriff," the receptionist interrupted over the intercom of the phone on the desk. "US Marshal Will Draper is on the line for you."

The sheriff raised an eyebrow and looked to Nick. "Anything you want to change about your story before I take that call?"

"No, ma'am. But I would ask that you put it on speaker and refrain from mentioning that we're here."

"How about we start by putting it on speaker and see how it goes?"

A quick nod from Nick. "Your house, your rules."

Lori's stomach flipped over and knotted.

"Sheriff Holmes, here. How can I help you, Marshal Draper?"

"Hello, Sheriff. I have reason to believe that a rogue deputy of mine, Nick McKenna, along with a witness who is in protective custody, is on his way to see you. If he's not there already."

One silent beat passed, followed by another as the sheriff eyeballed Nick. "What makes you think that, Marshal?"

"The transceiver in his car shows that he's very close to your location," Draper said. "A quick stroll away."

Sheriff Holmes tilted her head, gaze bouncing between Nick and Lori.

Nick clenched his jaw and Lori could tell he was beating himself for leaving the car so close. But it wasn't as if they'd had time to switch cars and she hadn't been up for a trek through the woods on foot. The longer they were exposed in public, the easier it would be for Belladonna to find them.

Lori wanted to reach over and take his hand, tell him that it was okay.

"You said Deputy McKenna has gone rogue. In what way?" Sheriff Holmes asked.

"He just lost his partner and has faced several near-death experiences today."

That was all true, Lori thought. Maybe Draper wasn't

the traitor and had no intention of throwing Nick under the bus.

"But McKenna has shown signs of being unstable," Draper said, shattering Lori's fragile hope. "I'm afraid this has sent him off the rails."

Lori shook her head, wordlessly pleading with the sheriff not to believe a word of it, but Draper went on.

"First, he violated protocol, endangering a very important witness by taking her to be treated at a veterinary clinic," Draper said, and the sheriff's eyes flared wide. "Then he abandoned his government-issued phone. He's paranoid, delusional and exhibiting rash behavior."

"You son of a bitch." Nick jumped to his feet. "You're just trying to cover your own ass. Isn't that right, Mr. Clean?"

"Listen to me, you hotheaded, impulsive, insubordinate bastard," Draper said.

"Which veterinarian?" Sheriff Holmes interrupted, her face darkening with alarm.

Draper didn't respond, and Nick hung his head.

The sheriff stood up. "I asked which clinic." Her voice was cold steel.

"Happy Paws and Wagging Tails," Lori said. Regret and guilt snaked through her veins. "Your daughter's clinic."

Sheriff Holmes blanched.

"Draper, you still there?" Nick's brow furrowed. "Draper?"

The sheriff picked up the receiver, putting it to her ear, paused, then stabbed a few buttons on the dialer. "The line is dead."

Lori and Nick turned toward the front door at the same time.

Four black SUVs pulled up and parked.

Lori's stomach dropped to the floor. "Oh, God. They're here."

Chapter Ten

"Who's here?" Sheriff Holmes asked.

"The cartel." Nick drew his weapon. "They're here for Lori." *Draper strikes again.* Nick and Lori had to make it through this alive, so he could beat Draper to a bloody pulp.

A deputy walked in from the back door next to the sheriff's office. He ducked his head inside the room. "Hey, Aunt Sheila—I mean Sheriff. As I was coming in, I noticed a suspicious van and SUV pull up out back."

The sheriff hopped to her feet. "Suzie! Lock the front door. Now!"

The receptionist wrenched open a desk drawer and fished out a set of keys. She scurried out of her seat and hustled to the door. Fumbling with the keys trying to find the right one, she dropped them, and they fell to the floor in a clatter. She scooped them up and scrabbled for the right one. Shoving the key into the dead bolt, she locked it.

Suzie clutched the keys to her chest and backed away from the doors.

The deputy looked around, his eyes clouded with confusion. "What's going on, Auntie?"

"The *Los Chacales* cartel is here."

"The Jackals? Are you kidding me?" He rocked back

on his heels. "What are they doing around here? Vacationing at the lake?"

"No, Denny," the sheriff said, flatly.

"Wow." He folded his arms. "You're serious."

"Nick, what do we do?" Lori asked.

Belladonna exited one of the vehicles, walked up to the front door, slipped her hands into her pockets and waited.

Nick reached out and drew Lori close, putting her behind him. "We need to prepare for heavy action."

"Denny, go to the armory," Holmes said. "See if you can contact the State Police on the two-way radio. Then bring everything you can carry, locked and loaded—extra ammo, too."

"I can help you carry weapons," Lori said.

Nick nodded for her to go with him. "But stay away from windows."

"There are none back there," the deputy said. "Come on, miss."

"That woman is called Belladonna." Nick gestured to the dark-haired, lethal-looking lady out front. There wasn't a stitch of concern on her face. The air of confidence about her was unnerving. "She's not here to talk. She's here to kill Lori Carpenter. Anything she says or does is with that singular goal in mind."

Sheriff Holmes nodded. "That may be, but this is my house. My rules. And we'll play it my way."

Nick followed the sheriff to the receptionist's desk. "Suzie, if I give the signal, you hit the emergency button. Understand?"

The receptionist's gaze flickered to a big red button on the wall next to her desk, then she looked back to the sheriff and nodded. "I understand."

"Then what happens?" Nick asked. "A bunch of flares launch, and someone responds to the distress signal?" He wasn't trying to be funny, but he did want to know how the red button was going to save the day.

"No flares. This place gets locked down tighter than a chastity belt with four-inch-thick reinforced steel, capable of withstanding the impact of a truck. Nobody is getting in."

He wished he shared her confidence, but Belladonna was full of surprises, and underestimating her might be a mistake they wouldn't live long enough to regret.

"No joy on the two-way, Aunt—" Denny stammered. "I mean Sheriff," he said, setting down an armful of weapons on one of the desks in the rear of the station. He had everything from assault rifles, shotguns, to M84 stun grenades. But the last item he dropped on the table was unexpected.

"You have a machete?" Nick asked.

Denny grinned and nodded. "We confiscated it two months ago from a hunter going after big game in the area without a license. I shudder to think what he planned to do with it. Hack up a mountain lion or a bear?" Grimacing, he shrugged.

Lori dumped boxes of extra ammo beside the stash.

"Hang back there," Nick said to her, not wanting to give Belladonna the chance to take a potshot at Lori or give a possible sniper a clear line of sight.

Pressing her palms to the bulletproof vest, Lori gave a quick nod.

"What's the plan?" the deputy asked.

"That woman is standing there waiting to talk," Holmes said. "So I'm going to hear her out and make it clear that Ms. Carpenter is under the protection of this department. Then I'll take it from there."

"I'd advise against talking to Belladonna at all, much less winging it." Nick didn't think the sheriff was being naive, assuming it would be quite that simple, but she was way out of her depth here. "Dealing with the cartel isn't the same as handling a few meth heads or some drunks in a bar fight."

"This may be a small town, but I'm not a dumb hick. And this is my house." The sheriff looked at Suzie. "If it comes to it, on my mark, hit the button. Don't hesitate."

"I won't let you down, Sheriff," Suzie said.

Holmes squared her shoulders and straightened her spine like she was shoring herself up. She turned and pulled open the inner door, stepping into the vestibule.

Nick kept his weapon ready and stood on the threshold between the small antechamber and the rest of the station so he could hear the conversation and cover the sheriff.

With his gun aimed at Belladonna, he wondered if chopping off the head would stop the war-beast hunting Lori. Or would two new heads spring up?

Belladonna clasped her hands in front of her as if preparing to do business. "Good day, Sheriff."

"*Los Chacales* aren't welcome in my town. What do you want?" Holmes asked through the door.

"I think you know the answer to that question already." Belladonna's gaze cut to Nick before falling back to the sheriff.

"It's not going to happen," Holmes said. "You'll have to go through me, my deputy and that deputy marshal in there first to get to that woman. Not to mention the State Police who'll show up if you start any trouble and cause problems. It isn't worth it. I suggest you get back in your vehicle and leave with the rest of your *Jackals*."

"I'm willing to wager you'll open that door for me within the next two minutes."

The sheriff hooked her thumbs on her utility belt. "I'll take that bet and double down."

"I like your spirit." An amused look spilled across Belladonna's face. She glanced at her wristwatch, then lifted her hand and snapped her fingers.

The rear passenger's side door of the SUV on the right opened. A man got out, tugging someone along with him.

Renee. She was alive.

A jolt of relief that the young veterinarian hadn't been killed was quickly submerged in a wave of dread. Gut-churning, get-a-head-start-running, they-were-screwed dread.

Belladonna had the ultimate leverage.

"Renee?" the deputy asked, stepping closer.

A harsh audible breath rushed from Sheriff Holmes. Her hands flew to the door, palms pressed to the glass. "Oh, God, not my baby," she said in barely more than a whisper, her voice cracking.

As the sheriff's composure dissolved from staunch professional into terrified parent, that sense of dread morphed into something deeper, scarier. His instincts might be misfiring, and maybe he was overreacting. It was possible that Sheriff Holmes was so principled that her response would be aboveboard.

But Nick was no idiot. It was possible, but not probable. Renee was gagged and her hands bound, but didn't appear to have any injuries. Her tearstained faced looked younger, more innocent, than it had an hour ago.

Belladonna took Renee by the elbow and hauled her up to the door. "Sheriff, I understand that you have an admirable sense of duty and a moral constitution that I never will, but nonetheless respect. You can keep your principles, your conscience unsullied. Or your daughter can keep her life."

A sob came from Sheriff Holmes and she covered her mouth with her hand.

"Don't do it, Mom," Renee said, the words muffled but the meaning crystal clear. "Don't."

"If you listen to your daughter, tomorrow you'll be planning her funeral. Deciding between a casket and cremation." Belladonna's grave words hung there.

The tension stretching throughout the station pulled tight as a rubber band ready to snap.

"Aunt Sheila, it's Renee, for crying out loud," the deputy said, trying to get closer, but Nick raised a palm, keeping him back. "We've got to open it, don't we?"

Trembling, Holmes shook her head, like it was an impossible choice ripping her apart on the inside. Nick could only imagine what was going through her mind.

His gut twisted with worry.

Sheila Holmes was an upstanding sheriff, but she was a mother first. A mama bear who wasn't going to let anyone hurt her cub. To hell with the law. To hell with having blood on her hands. To hell with aiding and abetting murderers.

Nick had from that very moment until the sheriff admitted the very same to herself for him to figure out what to do.

The wall clock ticking into the petrified silence told him he didn't have long.

"If you open that door," Nick said, "Lori is dead, and the Jackals win. More people will die at their hands."

"Lori's testimony may hurt the flow of our money for a little while, but it will *not* stop us. More people will die at our hands regardless." Belladonna was all business. "If you don't open the door, I'll snap your daughter's neck like a twig, and I promise you that I will still get inside your station. You'd gain nothing, and lose your daughter for what? To protect Lori Carpenter, a woman who isn't as innocent and sweet as she might lead you to believe."

Lori's eyes had grown wider and wider as the assassin had spoken.

Belladonna's gaze flashed past the sheriff and collided with Nick's. In his peripheral vision, he saw Lori backpedaling away.

"A year is a long time to spend watching over someone. Isn't it, McKenna? Easy to understand if you've developed a soft spot for her. Did she tell you how she became the accountant for WCM's largest client?"

"Her in-laws own the firm," Nick said. "She was given the promotion as part of the settlement of her divorce." They'd both been briefly married before. He'd gleaned tidbits from their conversations about their exspouses, but that was as much as Lori had shared. Deflecting with how she couldn't discuss the case.

"Is that what she told you? And, of course, you believed her. It's a good story. Not as sordid as the truth. Did she happen to mention that she was my boss's lover for almost a year?"

It was a blow, hitting Nick in the chest like a sucker punch.

"Oh, yes." Belladonna nodded. "They were hot and heavy, lived together, your Lori and a *jefe* of *Los Chacales.* When the accountant handling our portfolio *retired*, my boss is the one who saw to Lori's advancement. He gave her quite a lot. A promotion. Jewelry. Luxurious trips. Payoffs. She took all of it. Including our hush money. To say the least, he's not happy with her. You're protecting a liar. A thief. A traitor. The mistress of a drug lord."

His heart stopped for a beat. Nick stood there, reeling, his head hung low. A part of him had suspected that Lori was hiding something. But this…

This was too ugly. Too repugnant. Too much.

He had to detach, be all focus and purpose. Not take the bombshell personally.

Nick looked up and caught the smirk on Belladonna's face.

This was what she wanted. To drive a wedge between them. Divide and conquer.

"You're very good," Nick said to Belladonna. "Quite silver-tongued."

"Thank you. I had an excellent teacher."

"But it won't work." Nick shook his head, clinging to cautious hope that none of this would influence the sheriff.

"Really?" Belladonna's face softened and her voice lowered as her gaze returned to Holmes. "This is a small town, Sheriff. No one will know that you opened the door. No one will care because Renee will still be alive."

Nick's pulse quickened, his body registering the

fight-or-flight need. "Lori may be all of the things you said. Hell, most of the people in WITSEC are, but she is still a material witness."

Justice had to prevail.

"Sheriff," Belladonna said, "what's it going to be? Lori Carpenter? Or your daughter? You have ten seconds."

"I can't do this." Holmes looked back at Nick and Lori over her shoulder, her expression stricken, her voice anguished. "Forgive me." She reached for her keys that were hooked on her belt.

Damn. Nick had expected it, but shock still slammed into him. He spun, vaulting toward the wall, and lunged for the red button.

He slapped it as hard as he could.

Steel shutters dropped in front of the door and windows, zipping down with a deafening thud.

"No! Renee!" Sheriff Holmes cried. "That's my daughter out there!"

Nick's gut burned. Renee Holmes was an innocent, only guilty of helping them. The last thing he wanted was to throw her to the wolves twice. "I'm sorry."

The shutter rattled as though someone on the other side had kicked it. "Pull it up!" Belladonna said.

"I can't," the sheriff sobbed. "It's on a thirty-minute time lock and sends an automatic distress signal to the State Police. Please, don't hurt my daughter! Please! Renee!" The sheriff sobbed, screamed, pounding on the door.

Her nephew rushed into the vestibule and threw his arms around her. From her trembling mouth came more wild, primal cries as she kicked and flailed.

Nick stood there, stunned to silence. The outpouring

of her pain was worse than if he'd taken physical blows on his head and shoulders.

Lori turned away from the sight, hugging herself, and leaned against the desk.

Five minutes ago he would've gone to Lori and put a reassuring hand on her back. Now, renewed shock and anger flooded his mind, churning and growing into something so raw he wasn't sure he could ever stand to touch her again.

This is just a job. She is just a witness.

And he'd keep telling himself that until it was true.

Denny dragged his aunt away from the door. Suzie went to her, as well. The two of them tried to console Holmes with words; they tried to comfort her by holding her, but nothing worked to stop her tears.

Once the sheriff's movements slowed and she caught her breath, she stared at Nick, glaring daggers at him. "What did you do?"

It was a rhetorical question, but in a low voice, he said, "Stopped you from making a terrible mistake."

"You son of a bitch." She lunged for him as though she meant to claw his eyes out.

Nick swung his gun in her direction.

Her nephew wrangled her back. "Aunt Sheila, don't. Please, calm down."

"Trying to save my daughter wasn't a mistake! Are you a parent, McKenna?"

The combination of the sheriff's tormented tone and the reality that he'd never had anything in his life as precious as a child gutted Nick. "No. No, I'm not."

Shaking her head, she squeezed her eyes shut and sobbed. Suzie hugged her back, crying along with her.

Everything the marshals had taught him kicked in.

"Sheriff, they have nothing to gain by hurting Renee now." It was the only thing Nick could think to say. His point was valid, but he didn't have a clue whether Renee would be unharmed. "She'll be okay," he said, using that well-practiced, comforting tone.

It wasn't his intention to make false promises. Witnesses fretted all the time about loved ones that had been left behind and needed reassurance. Sometimes hope had to be enough when there was nothing else to cling to.

"What if you're wrong," the sheriff snapped, "and they kill her out of spite? Those merciless monsters don't even need a reason to shed blood, but you gave them one. Didn't you? You ticked that woman off and she's going to take it out on my baby." She cut her eyes from him in disgust.

If he was wrong, and he prayed that he wasn't, then Renee's death would be on his conscience and he'd have to find a way to live with that.

"Lori, remove the sheriff's and deputy's sidearms," he said while keeping his gaze on the distraught mother.

"You can't do that," the nephew said.

Nick gestured for Lori to get on with it. She removed both guns from their hip holsters.

"It's just until you calm down." Incensed people in great distress did the stupidest things. Sometimes when they came to their senses, they had no recollection of what they'd done. "I think you should go back into your office and try to see reason." Nick motioned for them to start walking, keeping the gun pointed at them.

The trio shuffled to the office and Nick followed, to be certain no one made an irrational grab for one of the loaded guns on the table along the way.

"All we have to do is stay calm and wait it out," Nick said. "The cavalry will be here in less than thirty minutes."

DAMN!

Belladonna roared on the inside, thirsting to rip Nick McKenna's head from his body with her bare teeth. She'd been so close, so damn close, to sealing the deal and getting the sheriff to cooperate that her damn pulse throbbed in her temples.

Her first inclination was to exorcise the rage and frustration by shooting Renee in the face.

Then Belladonna thought of losing her own daughter to senseless violence, no open casket… Did she still have the nerve to do this job?

But it was more than just a trade. It was a culture of brutality.

Robin Leach never would've hosted a show called *Lifestyles of the Fierce and Dangerous.*

She needed to find a way out, for the sake of her family.

Love had planted seeds, taken root deep, and over the past three years, she'd sprouted a deplorable heart. It made her weak. Soft.

But in this moment, her determination was on fire.

She shoved Renee to the side. The young woman tripped and fell. Belladonna kicked at her to get going, but Renee cowered like a miserable, beaten dog.

Pulling on a tight, stoic expression, as if this fiasco didn't faze her in the least, Belladonna spun on her heel and crossed the street.

While her men backed up their vehicles, repositioning near her, she touched her earpiece. "Converge on my location. Now," she said to her people who were stationed at the rear of the building.

She was done playing games. The pressure was about to get cranked to the max.

Once her men poured out of their vehicles, armed to the nth degree, and huddled around her, she looked at Smokey. "Go get Big Ben."

He turned and marched to the van, like a loyal soldier.

"The State Police will be here in less than nine minutes," Belladonna said to the rest. "We need to get in there and eliminate the target in eight. On my mark, set your timers. In five. Four. Three. Two. One."

A series of digital beeps resounded.

Smokey returned carrying an anti-tank rocket launcher loaded with a high-explosive warhead. He propped it on his shoulder, aimed at the sheriff's department and prepped the RPG.

Across the street, Renee's eyes flared wide. She scrambled up from the ground and took off like a bat out of hell.

Finally. *Stupid bitch.*

With the snap of her fingers, Belladonna issued the wordless order, *Smokey, make a hole.*

He smirked. "My pleasure."

Chapter Eleven

Darkness. Lori's head swam in a sea of darkness.

Her eyelids fluttered open. She lay facedown, her cheek pressed against the tile floor. Dust and acrid smoke tainted each breath, clogged her throat.

Her ears rang above the pounding in her head. Her lungs were like heavy, wet sandbags. She coughed, barely able to breathe, the throbbing ache remaining.

Nick!

A terrifying blast had torn through the front of the sheriff's department. The intensity of the explosion had hit the building like a magnitude-ten earthquake. Nick had grabbed her and shoved her down behind a desk. She would've sworn he'd been right there beside her.

Nick!

She wanted to move, to find Nick. But it was as if she'd been displaced from her body and had no control over her limbs.

On a primitive level, she knew she had to get up— had get out of there. But her brain was full of static, blaring white noise.

One thought broke through. Belladonna was coming for her. That assassin wouldn't stop until Lori was dead and permanently silenced.

Her mind staggered at the grim reality.

She had to move. Now. Lori mustered her strength and pushed up to her knees. The movement made her head spin and her sluggish body ache in places that had been numb a moment ago.

"I've got you." Nick clutched her shoulders, his voice bringing instant comfort.

He was alive.

"Can you stand?"

She had to try. "Think so."

Holding her by the arms, he hauled her onto her feet. Her chest heaved with the harshness of her strained breathing.

Pain ripped through her side and she pressed her palm to the area. It was tender and sore.

Lori swayed and staggered, desperate to orient herself. "What happened?"

"My best guess, it was an RPG. We have to move before they come in and slaughter us all. The smoke and the flames at the front are the only reasons that they aren't already in here."

His words were the adrenaline-fueled shot of reality that she needed. Survival instinct kicked in, jumpstarting her brain and snapping her out of a stupor.

She gave a weak nod and turned to him. His appearance rattled her. Plaster dust and ash covered him, his face peppered with cuts and bruises, but he was alert. Closer inspection made her freeze. Blood dripped from his temple down along his cheek. The breath locked in her lungs. She touched a gash on his head above his brow.

He hissed in pain, reeling away from her fingers.

The sound gripped her heart, reminding her of the

secrets Belladonna had spilled and twisted. Not into lies, but into an oversimplified, convenient version of the truth.

"Nick, are you okay?"

His lips thinned, the look in his eyes savage. "Yeah, I'm fine," he said in an uncompromisingly male tone. "You?"

Her skin was hot and damp with perspiration, and every muscle throbbed like a wound. "I'm walking and talking, so yeah. I guess." She looked around.

There were too many things to register at once. Plaster was still crumbling around them. Ashes rained down. Sparking electrical wires hung from the ceiling. Everything was in ruins—shattered glass, twisted steel, chunks of concrete. The reinforced shutter that had been shielding the front door was decimated. A gaping hole ringed by a jagged line of fire was left in its wake.

Nick rushed to the far rear of the station and checked on the others inside the sheriff's office. Lori tried to catch her breath and stayed close behind him, battling the dizziness.

The sheriff, the deputy and the receptionist were in shock, but managed to climb to their feet.

Suzie's bleeding arm appeared to be the worst of their injuries, but she didn't look too good. She swayed, unable to find her balance.

Lori wondered if she might have a concussion. Hell, they all might.

Suzie doubled over and vomited.

That wasn't good. The receptionist needed medical attention.

"We've got to pull it together, quickly," Nick said to the room. "Time is the enemy and it's working against us."

The deputy hurried and made sure his aunt was okay.
Once she nodded and waved him off, Denny grabbed
Suzie's arm, slung it over his shoulders, and helped
steady her.

"They're about to storm in here and kill everyone."
Nick's tone was as grave as their situation. "We need
to be ready. In position to open fire first and not let
them in."

"No!" The sheriff shoved off her desk and pushed
forward. "We can't use lethal force. What if Renee is
still alive and they use her as a human shield? Or she
could get hit by a stray bullet. We can't fire unless we
have clear shots."

The possibility of Renee taking friendly fire hadn't
occurred to him. The idea was more than he could swallow. He'd left her to hang out to dry twice already. This
wasn't going to be the third time. If she was alive out
there, then he'd take every precaution to see that she
wasn't harmed. He owed her for how she'd helped them
when she didn't have to.

"All right," Nick said. "With all the smoke and dust,
the only way to get a clear shot is to go outside, which
might work to our advantage better than staying cor-
nered and letting those murderers pick us off one by
one." He went to the stockpile of weapons on the table
a few feet away. Slinging a rifle over his shoulder, he
also took the machete. "I'll start with nonlethal force."
He snatched the stun-grenade launcher from the table
and held it up. "The rest of you, arm up."

Propelled by a sense of urgency and self-preservation
to evade, to escape, they each grabbed weapons.

Lori took two handguns and made sure the safety

was off. Nick had taught her the basics of gun safety, even though they'd never practiced shooting.

If her skill at carnival shooting gallery games was any indication of her skill level, then her aim was lousy. But she reasoned that if someone got close enough, she'd be able to put a bullet in them.

"Okay, move it, people." Nick gestured and it got them all in gear, shuffling along. "We've got to hurry."

They made their way through rubble toward the front of what was left of the station. Stumbling around a block of concrete, Lori narrowly avoided an electrical wire that dropped and sizzled when it hit the floor.

Nausea bubbled in her stomach, but she kept going, hurrying along. One step in front of the other.

At the ragged, charred entrance, they separated and dispersed on either side. They all crouched down low behind what walls were left, staying out of sight. The billowing smoke and falling ash helped to camouflage them.

"I know it's called a stun grenade, but will it be strong enough to slow them down and give us a chance?" Lori asked.

Nick took her hand, his thumb brushing over her skin, and just as quickly let go as if he'd touched an exposed electrical wire. The spark of awareness hit her hard and deep. Then his gaze turned glacial, his features shuttering.

She wished they had thirty seconds alone, hardly enough time to explain how complicated things were for her, but enough to apologize for disappointing him. For hurting him by not being a better person.

"Each grenade will issue a flash of around six million candela—a huge pyrotechnic charge that will cause immediate blindness—and one hundred eighty decibels that will render them deaf. It'll knock them on their butts for a few minutes and give us a shot." He looked to the sheriff, letting Lori's hand go, and she rubbed her palm, surprised by the residual tingle. "Getting outside is the only way to see what's what. Right after I unleash a can of fury, or rather three, we make a break for it. We'll have minutes at best. Seconds at worst. We'll need to make each and every one count."

"Everybody watch your aim, in case Renee is out front," Sheriff Holmes said, and the group nodded in response. "You two should take off, get out of town. No offense, but if you leave, then maybe the trouble will follow you."

The sheriff wasn't wrong, and Lori wasn't offended. The trouble, aka Belladonna, would most certainly follow them.

"Fair enough," Nick said in response. "But we won't get far on foot. Does anyone have a car we can use?"

"I do." Denny fished keys out of his pocket and tossed them to Nick. "My Bronco is parked out back. It's an old beater, but it runs."

Nick gave a nod of thanks and stuffed them in his pocket. Turning, he took a knee and peeped around through the opening.

"Damn. They're coming across the street," he said low, raising the hair on the back of Lori's neck.

Her pulse skyrocketed, beating too fast, adrenaline soaring in her blood. She could do this. She had to do this. No other choice.

He lifted the launcher, lowered his eye to the sights and pulled the trigger. Three cans discharged with a soft *pssh* sound.

"Everyone, take cover," he whispered.

A hard lump of ice dropped in her gut, blipping out the nausea. Lori pressed her back against the wall. She closed her eyes and covered her ears.

THE CLATTERING SOUND was soft, barely perceptible over the car alarms blaring in *dee-do, dee-do* succession. The others had missed it. Three small canisters that had dropped, rolling on the asphalt in front of them. Putting them dead center in the kill radius of the grenades.

But Belladonna was several paces behind them and saw it.

She turned and shouted, "Grenade!" as she ran and dove for cover behind a nearby pickup truck. But it was too late to save them.

Brilliant flashes of light erupted behind her and at the same time two-hundred-decibel teeth-rattling bangs cracked the air.

Flash-bangs designed to disorient and confuse anyone in the vicinity. Not high-yield explosive or incendiary grenades meant to kill.

This was law enforcement she was dealing with. Stun grenade should've been her first thought, and if it had been, she would've covered her ears. But she had reacted on pure instinct.

She had been turned away from the flashes and had shut her eyes the second she processed what was happening, sparing her retinas the worst of it. Her vision was a little blurred and she saw stars.

Her ears were a different story. Forget about hearing at all.

The concussive blasts and deafening bangs turned

her brain to mush. Ruptured her tympanic membrane. Disrupted the fluid in her middle and inner ear.

She tried to stand. The ground became a Tilt-A-Whirl ride, her balance obliterated.

Before she looked at her men, she knew what she'd find. The agonizing bursts of light had fried their eyes and since they had been farther ahead of her, they had absorbed the full brunt of the brain-hammering pops.

She peered around the rear of the truck. Her rooks and bishops were disabled and useless, writhing on the ground, holding their heads. Easy pickings.

Smokey and another rook were the closest to her. Both outweighed her by a good one hundred pounds. She grabbed Smokey by the collar and heaved with all her might, dragging him behind the vehicle.

Daring to go for the other one, she snatched his arm and hauled him across the pavement. Everything was off center and spinning. She stumbled and fell. There was no shaking off the effects of the stun grenades. She just had to muddle through it until the brain-caught-in-a-blender side effect wore off. Gripping her rook by both his wrists, she heaved again.

It wasn't team spirit and it certainly wasn't compassion that spurred her on.

Replacing them wouldn't be simple or easy. The more she had to do on her own, the more risks she'd have to take, and the less likely she'd be to survive this assignment.

She was acting out of sheer practicality.

Nick McKenna was the first one to emerge from the smoke and ashes of the building, a semiautomatic rifle at the ready. Lori Carpenter was behind him, wielding a gun in each hand.

What was this? The OK Corral?

McKenna opened fire. There was only a high-pitched ringing in her ears, but the flashes from the muzzle were unmistakable. She registered the gunfire as distant muffled thuds. Each one she felt more than heard as it resonated through her.

Two of her men on the ground stopped moving. Shot and killed.

Panting, she released the second rook, content that his head and torso were out of danger of being hit by a stray bullet.

She took a beat to recover her breath and duckwalked toward the hood of the pickup.

Her vision had cleared. She didn't see white spots fading in and out any longer. Belladonna drew her suppressed 9mm and rose. The world still seesawed and her gun hand shook. Lining up her sights, she aimed for Lori Carpenter's forehead and pulled the trigger. Her HK VP9 snapped twice, and she took comfort in the familiar recoil if not the sound.

A bullet struck the target.

In the damn vest, of all places.

The force of the projectile knocked Lori Carpenter backward and she dropped.

McKenna trained the barrel of his rifle on Belladonna and opened up on her.

She ducked behind the truck.

With the loss of her hearing and the disruption of the fluid in her ears, Belladonna's equilibrium was toast. Her normally perfect aim had been thrown way the hell off, but this was ridiculous. She'd had the woman in her sights and only caught her in the chest near the collarbone.

The target had fallen from the impact, but the vest had taken the bullet, and Lori Carpenter was still alive.

A red haze of fury filmed Belladonna's vision, anger flooding her limbs like battery acid. This wasn't what she needed right now. Her eyesight was the one thing going for her and she needed to get a grip.

She cursed her luck and checked her watch. Four and a half minutes left. The game was still on.

The target would be dead weight. McKenna would have to carry her. And he wouldn't be able to fire behind him at the same time.

Taking a breath, she took her chances and stood.

Precisely as she'd forecasted, McKenna had the target slung over his shoulder and was hightailing it east.

She leveled her gun at them, took a steady breath, strained to focus the sights on Carpenter's dangling head and—

The truck windshield in front of her exploded, struck by a fusillade of bullets that drove her down behind the frame of the vehicle.

She pivoted and peered around to see the sheriff, Deputy Barney Fife and Aunt Bee taking potshots at her as they maneuvered down Main Street.

In what upside-down world was she playing defense instead of being on the offense?

Not the OK Corral, but *The freaking Andy Griffith Show*!

If she wasn't worried about getting shot, she'd look around for Ashton Kutcher to jump out and say, "You've been punk'd."

The trio was headed in the opposite direction from McKenna and the target, but Belladonna would have to expose herself to have another go at Carpenter.

She growled her frustration, preparing to do something reckless and impulsive, totally against the grain, when her men started to recover enough to shoot back and lay down suppressive fire.

Before she could draw a relieved breath, the second rook she'd saved lurched back and twisted like a spinning top, falling on top of her and knocking her to the ground.

Blood poured from his face. His cheek had a gruesome hole in it. He was a goner and nothing could be done for him, but even worse, he was leaking all over her, getting her filthy and leaving the worst mess.

This was a DNA nightmare that housekeeping wouldn't have time to clean.

They needed to pull the plug on this gunfight and get back on point, tracking the target.

She shoved the corpse to the side and sprang to her feet. Catching the eyes of Smokey and a handful of the others, she motioned for them to follow her. She returned fire as they fled, but the three locals, who'd ended up being an effective distraction, slipped inside an establishment.

Glancing around, she counted four men dead and two more wounded. McKenna and the target were nowhere to be seen.

They'd gone east but couldn't have gotten far. Especially on foot. McKenna's car was still parked two doors down. They'd go for a new vehicle.

She checked the time. Two minutes until the State Police arrived on the scene.

Gritting her teeth, Belladonna and her team split up into two different SUVs. They would find the target and McKenna.

They weren't called *Los Chacales* for nothing.

Jackals were fast, deadly hunters, and the primary reason they weren't an endangered species was because of their resourcefulness.

Chapter Twelve

The hustle to the Bronco left Nick winded. He got Lori into the passenger side and climbed in behind the wheel. Keeping his Glock holstered, he chucked the rifle and machete in the back to get them out of the way. They hit the seat and floor in a clatter. He cranked the engine, backed around and hit the gas. Heart pounding off the rails, he sped out of the parking lot behind the sheriff's department, the tires squealing.

He checked all his mirrors. Belladonna and her crew wouldn't be far behind. It was a small town. One way in and one way out. At least, as far as he knew. Only a matter of time before they found him, and he couldn't waste time looping around and backtracking. That would give the chance to form a roadblock and box them in.

Best to make a beeline straight out of town. The great race was on, but they were at a disadvantage in the beat-up, late-model Bronco. Flooring this thing to seventy might be pushing it past its limits.

He checked his mirrors again. All clear behind him.

Lori groaned, opening her eyes. She went to sit forward but winced and dropped back in the seat. The pain must've been excruciating.

In Afghanistan, he'd taken a bullet once. His vest had saved him, too, but his chest had ached for days.

"Can you take off the vest?" His gaze bounced between the road ahead and the road behind in the mirrors, and then over to Lori. "I need to make sure you aren't injured."

The slug had snapped Lori's body to the ground with such violent force, it was as though a steel fist had gripped his heart. The bullet had struck dangerously close to her throat. If Belladonna's aim hadn't been off, another couple of inches higher, and Lori would be bleeding out. But her collarbone could still be broken.

Nick made a sharp left turn, hit the next corner and made a right onto SR 18.

Removing the Velcro straps, Lori wheezed through the agony her poor body had endured today. She was taking it like a real trouper. No complaints. No whining.

"You okay?" she asked, groaning as she pulled the body armor overhead.

Lori's worrying about him when her clavicle might be broken and her chest must've been throbbing revealed another quality about her that he found endearing. He wanted to wipe his mind clean of the ugly things he'd learned. Turn back the clock to when she had been his Lori.

Not that she had ever really been *his*, but his heart didn't seem to realize it.

"Let me see," he said, pulling down the collar of her shirt and inspecting her with his fingers.

She winced, shrinking back from his touch. The blunt force of the bullet would leave a nasty bruise.

"It's not broken. But the area will start bruising soon."

"Where are we going? To meet up with your tactical teammates?"

Nick shook his head, gaze flickering to the rearview and side mirrors. "No. Doing so means putting you in the palm of Draper's hands." He trusted Yaz and Charlie with his life, but Nick didn't trust Draper as far as he could throw him. "He'd decide which San Diego safe house to put you in overnight and who'll be on your protective detail. Odds-on certainty that Draper will pull me."

Alarm crossed Lori's face. "I don't want that."

Neither did Nick. He gritted his teeth, wishing the only reason was to finish the mission.

"So what are we going to do?"

"Plan B. Or is this C?"

"Honestly, I think we're up to D." She flashed a sad, weak smile.

He clenched his fingers, resisting the urge to caress her cheek, and pulled the phone from his pocket. Most numbers he didn't know by heart, so used to having everything saved on his cell and at his fingertips. Other than the office, he had two other numbers memorized.

His mother's and his older brother's.

He dialed and was relieved when his call was answered on the third ring.

"Hello, this Bowen McKenna." His brother's voice, deep and powerful, the way Dad's had been, resonated over the phone.

"Hey, Bo. It's me."

"What kind of hot water are you in this time?"

Nick groaned. "Why would you assume I'm in trouble?"

"Because you call Mom when everything is fine," Bo said, "and you call me when you're in trouble."

Fair enough. "I need help."

"See. What do you need?"

"Airlift. Can you fly into Big Bear Airport, pick me and a witness up?"

"A witness? That sounds like a violation of USMS protocol."

"It's a long story, but I promise my reasons for asking are solid. If you don't do this, I'm pretty sure my witness won't live to see the sun rise." He exchanged a glance with Lori, and the trust in her eyes, the affection she had for him, shredded him. If he could just get through tomorrow, his life would go back to normal, the way it was supposed to, and this temptation, his anger, the gut-wrenching disappointment, would fade, and he could work on forgetting her. Reestablish the line in the sand that he'd never cross again. "And no guarantees that I'll make it, either."

"No pressure there." Bo chuffed a deep laugh. "You're lucky it's my day off. I'll get the helicopter fired up and head out. Is this a good number to reach you?"

"For now, anyway, yeah. Be sure to use Mom's maiden name for the logs. I don't want any record of a McKenna flying in and out."

"Got it. Be there as soon as I can."

He owed his brother one. Bo was the most reliable, dependable, bail-your-butt-out-no-matter-what person Nick knew. His brother never considered the blowback from helping, simply dove in and gave an assist whenever needed.

"And don't say you owe me one because you owe me like a million."

Nick smiled on the inside. "Who's counting, right? Thanks, Bo." He disconnected. "We'll spend the night in Nevada at my family's compound and fly into San Diego in the morning." Going totally dark was for the best. Too many coincidences and unanswered questions surrounding Draper.

His family was trustworthy. The compound was fortified. And they had a *working* relationship with the local law enforcement. Most important, no one in the USMS would know that they were there.

Hope bloomed in his chest. As he looked up in the rearview mirror again, that hope withered. He spied a hulking black SUV speeding up behind them. His fingers itched in warning. The road headed out of town was flat, and the SUV whipped around the sparse traffic in sight, eating up the asphalt and closing the distance.

"We're being followed."

Lori turned around and looked through the back windshield. "It's her. Isn't it? Belladonna, the damn terminator. She keeps coming and won't stop until I'm dead."

Protective instincts flared hot. "Well, she's going to have to come through me to get to you." He had to separate the personal from the professional, like church and state. "Because I won't stop until you've testified. Then you become some other deputy marshal's problem."

Lori sucked in a shaky breath, emotion burning in her eyes. "Right."

He hurt at the pain he saw in her features. Pain that he'd caused. But there was no time to worry about bruised feelings, not when the much higher priority was keeping them both breathing.

Letting out an irritated groan, he refocused.

When the SUV behind them cut around a minivan, he spotted two vehicles following them. Not one.

Great. The more, the deadlier.

The lead SUV roared up, eating the asphalt between them. If that beast of a vehicle was armored, they were screwed.

Nick gripped the wheel hard enough to make the leather groan, preparing for anything.

They crossed the town limits. He floored it, hitting seventy-five before the engine protested.

The SUV rammed them, jostling the truck forward.

A squeak of surprise left Lori's lips. "Oh, God. They're trying to run us off the road."

"No, they're not. But we'd be lucky if they did."

She shot him a perplexed look. "Huh?"

"If they wanted to run us off the road, they'd be alongside us."

The car raced closer. Rammed them again, this time hitting the left corner of the rear bumper, confirming his guess. Belladonna's team was executing the PIT maneuver—precision intervention technique—he had learned from Bo when he was on terminal leave from the army deciding between joining the family business and the US Marshals Service.

"They're trying to knock us into a spin and force us to a stop. Surround us from there."

"How is being run off the road better?" Her voice was frantic. "We could die in a crash."

"Could, yes, but—" Another hard ram interrupted him. "We'd have a chance of making a run for it. They force us to stop. Box us in. We're dead. There's no bullet-proof glass or armored plating on this vehicle. All they'd have to do is open fire to turn us into Swiss cheese."

"But what about all the stuff in the woods? Aren't there mountain lions, bears, snakes?"

"Better the wildlife in the woods than the Jackals behind us."

The SUV bulldozed up from behind to take another swipe at them. This time Nick hit the brakes. The anti-lock braking system kicked in. Then he cut the wheel hard to the right. The Bronco gave an ear-splitting squeal as the rear end fishtailed. Another ram from the SUV sent both vehicles into a wicked spin.

But their Bronco went spiraling off the road over to the left, sideways and downhill. The car flipped and bounced. The rough terrain of an embankment rushed up to greet them.

Down the car went again at a sharp angle and in a long, fast slide.

If not for the seat belt that cut into his chest and abdomen, he would've gone out the windshield. The car's frame shrieked as it contorted.

Metal grinding, glass shattered and imploded, the vehicle came to an abrupt halt as it slammed into a tree.

An airbag inflated, knocking him back in his seat. Dust saturated his airway. Dazed, he pulled his Glock and shot the deployed airbag. It deflated instantly. He looked over. Lori was in the same predicament. One bullet rectified the problem.

His brain kicked into gear. He processed that they were upside down.

The thought of time hit him next. They had no time.

Belladonna and her people would swarm down the hill as soon as possible.

He fumbled with the seat belt and depressed it. Bound by gravity, he dropped down to the roof of the car. His hands landed atop shards of glass. But he had to keep moving. No pain. No weakness. Driving forward no matter what.

Lori was conscious, but stuck. He helped unbuckle her, making sure to keep her hands out of the glass. The soles of her feet were already damaged from earlier. He'd spare her any further suffering that he could.

He kicked out what was left of the windshield, not simple in the cramped space, and steered her out. But he didn't follow right away. They needed weapons.

Turning back, he smiled at the one thing in their favor. With their being inverted, every weapon in the truck was on the roof in plain sight and he didn't have to scavenge for them.

He handed Lori his Glock. She seemed reasonably comfortable with a 9mm when she was shooting like Annie Oakley earlier, but she'd dropped both guns when the bullet hit her vest. "Here."

She took it and her gaze was drawn uphill. "Get out of the truck."

Nick slung the rifle over his shoulder, shoved another 9mm in the back of his waistband and grabbed the machete.

"Get out, Nick! Now!"

He crawled through the open windshield and scrambled to his feet.

At the top of the hill, a man stood on the crest of the embankment. A rocket launcher rested on his shoulder and he flipped up the sights.

Nick grabbed Lori's hand and they bolted into the woods. He shoved branches out of their way, guiding her under larger limbs as they wound around old, massive trees.

Behind them, a jarring explosion shook the ground. There was no need to look back to see that the Bronco was a ball of fire. Or to know that Belladonna's team was headed downhill after them.

Nick pulled Lori, forcing her tired feet to move faster. They were both exhausted, mentally and physically, but he prayed that adrenaline fueled her system hot as jet fuel, the same as his.

He wasn't sure how long they had until Belladonna's team dispersed and attacked from various flanks. They wouldn't all come head-on.

"Keep going. Head northeast."

Her eyes flared wide in alarm. Ragged breaths tore from her mouth. "No. We should stick together."

"We separate or we die."

"I'm slowing you down. Aren't I?"

She was. "No. If you keep going, then I can hang back and take a few of them. I swear to you, I'll catch up. I won't leave you alone. If you run into trouble, fire the weapon. I'll hear it. I'll come for you."

Lori's eyes were clouded with fear and doubt, but she nodded. "Don't die on me."

"I won't. Go!" he said in a harsh whisper, and Lori took off.

Nick repositioned the sling of the rifle across his body and slipped behind a redwood. Rotating his neck, letting the joints pop, he got ready for war.

Rangers were shock troops. Quick strike force and highly trained at capturing, securing and killing.

THE SKY HAD darkened to the point that you couldn't tell if it was dusk or day. Distant thunder rumbled. The air smelled of rain. And something bad.

Something close to failure.

Belladonna shrugged it off. Failure wasn't an option.

Her people had scattered, fanning out to encircle McKenna and the target. But Belladonna slowed her pace, hanging back a bit. She knew something the others didn't. McKenna's history. His military record.

He used to be a ranger. Trained to operate in mountains similar to these. Skilled in taking out the enemy in Iraq and Afghanistan, in someone else's backyard and at the disadvantage.

As if making her point for her, a bolt of lightning illuminated a wide, sharp blade swinging out, taking the head of the bishop twenty feet in front of her.

Belladonna raised her suppressed weapon and fired away. Bullets struck bark.

McKenna was gone. Vanished like a phantom.

Fat indigo clouds swelled on the horizon and the wind changed, along with her forecast.

On her right, she glimpsed McKenna dart out from behind a redwood, snap a neck and disappear again. Seconds passed. One of her men screamed thirty feet ahead. She was on the move, slinking around trees. By the time she got there, another bishop was down. In pieces.

McKenna was pretty good at killing. Too bad he wasn't on her team.

Alas, he worked for the opposition, and two kings couldn't remain on the same playing board much longer.

Movement on her left. A tortured scream. McKenna sliced through another like a searing blade through softened butter.

Her pulse kicked up, but her focus was laser sharp.

A breeze whispered past her. She spun three hundred

sixty degrees, ready to pop a cap in anyone who wasn't on her side.

Where the hell was Lori Carpenter? Squirreled away inside a hollowed-out tree trunk?

Belladonna wouldn't put it past McKenna.

She crept through the woods, tracking her quarry, determined to remain the hunter and not to become the prey.

Thunder roared, but over it a shot was fired. Wild and telling.

McKenna had been doing his best to remain silent, not using his government-issued gun that lacked a suppressor and would give away his position, opting for a machete instead. The target, Carpenter, had discharged the gun. A stupid civilian unaware of how the loud report would echo.

Belladonna took off in the direction of the shot at a controlled pace, eyes on the lookout for any booby traps, just in case it was an ambush. She wouldn't be the one ensnared.

Coming into a clearing, the light was dim. The sky dark.

Twigs snapped behind her. She pivoted and spotted one of her few remaining rooks. Her numbers were rapidly dwindling. She could execute any job on her own, but backup was better on an assignment such as this.

In the clearing she spotted McKenna, hacking away another of her brethren like a bloodthirsty butcher. Behind him the target stood, holding her neck, raking in air as if she'd come within inches of losing her life. Yet again.

Belladonna's teeth ached to make it happen and be done with this.

As she took aim, stepping into the meadow, McKenna spotted her.

Belladonna had them, finally, and she couldn't contain her smile.

Lori Carpenter gasped and reeled back. McKenna raised his hands, still clutching the bloody machete. Standing in front of the target and blocking a clean shot, he backed up, slowly, head lowered.

It was the oddest thing. Rather than reveling in the posture and cowered look, Belladonna's skin crawled.

A roar blasted behind her, rattling her to the marrow. It wasn't thunder. It was feral.

She pivoted, slowly, cautiously, training her weapon in the direction of the sound.

A black bear charged the rook behind her. He screamed and ran—toward her.

What the hell? It was every soul for themselves.

She wasn't an outdoorsy person and hated camping, but she'd picked up a thing or two. Never run from a bear.

Then it dawned on her that McKenna had spotted the animal and had responded to its presence, not to hers.

There was no time to check if McKenna and the target were still behind her—only a fool would be standing there. She took aim on the bear.

The charging beast swooped down on her rook. She fired. A claw ripped through the arm, connecting with human flesh. A double tap from her gun. Her rook's screams died. The bear growled and bellowed. Then it stormed toward her.

Her heart flew into her throat. Fear wasn't new. She embraced it, owned it and stood her ground. Taking a deep breath, she pulled the trigger twice.

The beast gave a whimper and dropped.

Belladonna whirled and took after McKenna and the target. She was a hunter, not a tracker, but she could tell what direction they had headed.

No matter the developments in her life, taking time off from work, becoming a wife and a mother, she'd never let herself go. She was in peak physical condition and could run a marathon if the mission necessitated it.

She leaped over a log and ducked under a low-hanging branch, her footfalls light and sure. Running all out at full speed, she'd trained herself not to take noisy breaths.

It paid off. She heard them.

One hundred feet ahead. Two running and a river—water rushing fast, something large. Not a babbling brook.

She wound around trees, sending little creatures scurrying. Faster. She needed to be faster and close the distance. Not let them slip through her fingers again.

Pumping her arms, driving her legs, ignoring the burn, she pushed even harder to close the distance. She glimpsed McKenna and Carpenter. This time, Carpenter wasn't wearing a vest.

They were hand in hand. Smart enough not to run in a straight line. They cut around a large redwood that obscured them.

Belladonna lengthened her stride, tasting victory on her tongue. Her heart pounded so hard, she thought it might explode. But she didn't care. There was only the chase. And her prey.

Her blood thudded against her eardrums. She was so close, could smell their sweat and fear in the air, the distant roar of the river amplifying the jolt firing in her muscles.

She burst through the tree line that opened onto a rugged dirt trail. Gun raised, vision clear, mind steady, the sweet rush of adrenaline singing in her veins.

They stopped to take a breath, and Belladonna stopped to take a shot, her finger on the trigger.

A twig snapped beneath her foot. The sound sent the two scurrying to the side and diving down a hill.

She took off after them, sprinting to the spot where they'd been standing only seconds ago. They skidded and tumbled in a wild descent down a steep grade. Belladonna squeezed off a few rounds, narrowly missing the target's head each time and hitting dirt, or rocks, or a damn tree.

Maybe Carpenter would break her neck on the way, or at least her leg to slow them down.

Belladonna redirected her aim, approximating where they'd stop. Have a steady, clean shot. The two reached the bottom, precisely where she'd calculated—as if landing on a marker—but soft earth gave way.

They both went in a violent whoosh as the river snatched them both, ripping them downstream.

Shock and frustration roiled hot through her, building and spiraling until it exploded. Belladonna screamed, raging at the air, at the storm coming in.

Taking a breath, she pulled in control. Battened down all emotion tight. They might drown. But *might* wasn't good enough. She needed Carpenter's head on a platter.

The river led somewhere. She'd find it. Then what?

They were hunters, not trackers. It wasn't the same thing at all.

There was also the possibility that McKenna and

Carpenter would find their way out of the water before they reached the mouth of the river.

Belladonna tapped her earpiece. "Who is left?"

Smokey was the first to respond, followed by two others. She'd started the day with fifteen. Now the target was in the wind.

Things couldn't get much worse.

Then her phone rang. She'd programmed a ringtone for anyone who might call this number. "Tubular Bells" played. The theme song for *The Exorcist*.

Her day just got worse.

Sucking in a calming breath, she answered the phone.

Chapter Thirteen

The shock of cold water exploded through Lori's body the instant they tumbled into the river. Icy water rushed into her and over her, stealing her breath. She flailed at the surface with her hands, trying to keep her head above water.

Nick was there, combating the current alongside her. One second they were close enough to almost touch. The next they were jostled apart. In this together but fighting their own separate war.

She went under, swallowing water, gagging. Lungs straining, near bursting. The current teasingly thrust her up. Her head popped out and she raked in a desperate breath. Keeping her chin above the surface was a battle she'd win and then lose.

The bank of the river was within reach. She struggled to grab at slippery rocks. To snatch hold of loose roots. But the current sent them hurtling downstream. Her fingers had no chance to find purchase.

She drew a breath, then another. The brutal assault was relentless. On a manic gasp for air, she took more water into her mouth. Her lungs. The weight of her clothing only dragged her down.

If she was still wearing the bulletproof vest, she would've surely drowned.

And she still might.

The rushing water sucked them both forward. Sheer momentum and the heavy current became the greatest threats.

"Branch!" Nick sputtered over the roar of the raging river, and it was a ferocious beast, more merciless than Belladonna.

She spotted it. A large branch that hung over the water. A lifeline.

The river tossed Nick into the lead, the current catapulting them faster and faster toward the fallen log. But they couldn't afford to miss it.

This was their only chance. The one possibility to get out.

Desperation beat through her hotter and harder than a pulse.

Almost there. Almost. *Now!*

Nick reached up, growling, revealing that he was pure warrior. Down to his soul. He snatched hold of the log.

With only seconds to reposition, he shifted and latched on to her jacket.

Hold on. Hold me!

She grabbed on to his arm and did her best to fight the current as he hauled her up to the log. They shimmied toward the bank. The river yanked insistently, clinging, like an angry lover that wouldn't let go.

The fallen branch was wedged into the bank. But with the two of them, their weight was too much. Spindly limbs snapped and broke. The soaked bark of the log began to crumble.

She clawed into the earth, grappling to find purchase, and this time her fingers did. Using what little strength she had left, she pulled herself up.

The branch gave way, falling to pieces. But she grabbed Nick's hand and tugged at him, her muscles burning and her neck straining from the effort.

Water beat against his body, making her temper flare. She pulled harder and helped drag him from the snarling current.

Her heart pounded against her ribs as she coughed up water and crawled over rocks and damp dirt and reeds to get as far from the bellowing river as her body would allow.

They both dropped on the ground. Soaked. Exhausted. Panting. But they were alive.

Huzzah!

She'd never had a greater sense of accomplishment. A stronger desire to jump up and dance for joy. But she was totally wiped.

"Now…what?" she asked between ragged breaths.

"We find the road. Avoid the Jackals. And hitch a ride."

Sounded like a plan.

"Ready?" He extended his hand to her.

Hell. No. She wasn't ready. Her limbs were heavy, and her lungs were finally starting to function properly again now that she'd expelled the water. Couldn't he give her one minute to catch her breath, revel in the fact that they hadn't drowned?

But she said, "Yeah. Let's go."

THE LIST OF reasons why Nick admired and, yeah, was crazy about Lori, had just gotten longer. Beautiful and

kindhearted, tough yet vulnerable, funny and coura-
geous, but she was also resilient. And girl-next-door
sexy. He'd never met a woman like her. Damn near
perfect.

Except for the other list of reasons that had landed
her in WITSEC. She was not a victim here. She was
a criminal.

He clenched his jaw and dropped her hand the second she was steady on her feet.

They were shivering from the cold and staggering
along like they'd been on a weeklong Vegas bender, but
he quickened his step. "Come on. Keep up. We've got
to find help and get out of these wet clothes."

Huffing and puffing, she held her own, matching him
stride for stride. Thankfully, they'd come across a trail.
It'd lead to the road or civilization. He'd take either.

They'd gone at least two miles before her lips turned
blue. First time that beautiful bow-shaped mouth of hers
had stayed closed for so long, leaving him to the torment of his conflicted thoughts.

"Thank you," she said, as if picking up on his need
to end the quiet. "For getting me out of the sheriff's department, away from Belladonna in the woods."

"No need to thank me. It's my job."

"If it hadn't been for you, things would've played
out a hell of a lot differently. Thanks for not turning
your back on me after what you heard, without knowing my side."

Now he had the torment of dealing with her thoughts.
The quiet would've been better.

"Your side?" he snorted. Her side of the lies, the be-
trayal. Her side of shacking up with a vile, despicable
man. Accepting his jewels, trips, payoffs, his hands

all over her body. His stomach roiled. The whole *sordid* thing sickened him. "You had a chance to come clean, tell me your version of the truth, and all about your kingpin sugar daddy. Instead, you clammed up and pulled away."

"Is that what you call your interrogation in the car? A chance?" Her angry eyes flashed up at him. "When I asked you to share who you are with me, I was calm, gentle, patient."

True, true, true. He growled on the inside. No way was he going to let her turn this around on him. He stopped and pinned her with a glare. "Before we walked into the sheriff's department, I was calm. And gentle. And as patient as you're ever going to get from me." He'd told her what was in his heart, only to have her reject it. "Still, you didn't say a word!"

She swallowed hard, her eyes watering, lips quivering. "Because I couldn't bear to put myself out there, peel back the layers, and have you look at me the way you are right now. Like you loathe the sight of me."

Guilt reared inside his chest. He clenched his jaw, not knowing what to say.

He could never loathe Lori. But he wasn't sure he could accept what she'd done, either.

A rumbling sound up ahead drew his attention. "Do you hear that?"

"Is it a truck?"

"Come on."

They ran down the trail, and through the tree line was a state highway. An eighteen-wheeler was just about to pass them, when Nick sprinted into the road on the lane opposite the oncoming truck and waved his hands. Lori ran up beside him and helped flag down the driver.

The truck passed them in a whoosh. Then the semi slowed to a stop.

They ran to the passenger side.

Nick climbed up, wrenched the door open and flashed his badge. "We could use a ride to the Big Bear Airport. It's official business and it'd be much appreciated."

"Sure! That's only a ten-minute detour. I don't mind helping you out."

They had a ride. Relief sliced through his chest.

Nick helped Lori up and inside.

The driver blasted the heater and gave them a blanket from the back.

"Very kind of you," Lori said.

The driver asked questions born of curiosity. It is to be expected when two people resembling drenched cats run into the middle of the road and one has a badge.

Nick gave brief, vague answers and luckily, the driver didn't push and the ride was short.

"Mind dropping us off here?" Nick said, gesturing to the tourist shop that sold souvenirs and clothing. The airport was only one block down.

"No problem." The driver came to a stop and let them out. "Good luck!"

"Thanks." They'd still need it.

The store was kitschy, crammed with cheap souvenirs, but they had dry clothes. Sweats were the simplest, warmest choice. Nick opted to keep his shoes on, even though they were soaking wet and squeaked. Lori picked flip-flops, not that there was much in the way of choices for footwear.

Nick set everything on the counter and threw in two pairs of sunglasses. "I've got limited cash. What kind of discount can you give?" he asked, once again flashing the badge like it was a black-and-white hypnotic spiral that could bend people to his will.

"I can offer a two-for-one law-enforcement deal."

He pulled out a few wet bills from his wallet. "Thanks, buddy," Nick said to the clerk.

Lori changed first in the single fitting room, and Nick went in after.

The clerk was kind enough to give them a large plastic bag for their stuff.

Dry, more or less, and reasonably warmer, they pulled on their hoodies and headed to the airport.

One city block. Six hundred and sixty feet. That was how far away the airport was. And all it'd take was for one Jackal to spot them and another exit strategy would go up in smoke and they'd be back on the run.

The hoodies and sunglasses helped disguise who they were, but at the same time it drew attention to them. An unavoidable trade-off.

Two hundred feet from victory, he spotted Charlie and Yaz leaving the airport and getting into a silver SUV parked out front waiting for them. They'd have to drive past Nick and Lori to go deeper into the town.

Nick grabbed Lori and shoved her into the doorway of a mom-and-pop bookstore. He tried the handle, but the door was locked. His gaze homed in on the be-back-in-15-minutes sign.

"What's wrong?" Lori asked.

"Deputy marshals. My guys are about to pass us."

"Why not talk to them, explain everything?"

They'd ask questions, doubt his plan, perhaps even

his sanity after he mentioned his concerns about Draper. Nick wasn't taking any more chances with Lori's safety. Draper be damned.

He pressed close to her, nudging them both into the corner. "It'd be a hell of a lot easier if they didn't spot us. We can just hang here a minute and pretend to be—"

Lori took Nick's face in her hands, and rising on her toes, brought his mouth to hers.

It wasn't a soft peck, but a greedy, openmouthed kiss that incinerated every thought in his head. Her tongue slid over his as her fingers dove into his hair. His lips burned and his body tingled. Without his permission, his mutinous arms wrapped around her, his treasonous hands clutching her closer.

He breathed her in, sucked down her flavor and squirmed to get even closer. The plains and valleys of their bodies fit and aligned like two halves of a whole. Before he realized it, he was the one deepening the kiss. Nick couldn't get enough of her mouth. The taste, the texture of her tongue, the sense of rightness despite the warning blaring in the recesses of his mind.

Need stirred inside him, an animate, living thing awakening with ravenous hunger.

His control was spinning, slipping away from him with each caress, each silken stroke of her tongue, and the only thing that mattered was the feel of her curled around him.

The sound of a throat clearing startled them, making them jump apart.

His heart jackhammered in his chest.

A thirtysomething woman with wide eyes and a wider smile, holding a takeaway coffee cup, jangled keys in front of them. "I can open up if you want to come in. But I kind of got the impression you two might prefer to be in a room at the B and B three blocks over." She waggled her eyebrows.

Lori blushed and hung her head.

"Sorry, ma'am." Nick took Lori's hand and led her away to the airport. "What were you thinking back there, kissing me like that?"

"I thought you wanted us to pretend to be intimate. You know, lovers, so no one would notice us. I was just trying to sell it."

Sold! He'd bought it lock, stock and barrel. "Don't do it again."

"You kissed me back, you know."

He wrenched the airport door open and carted her inside.

"You're hurting me," she said in a tight voice.

He looked down at their joined hands and only then did he register that he was not only holding her hand but also squeezing all the blood from her fingers. "Sorry." He let her go.

Pushing back his hood, he removed his shades, and she did likewise.

"Are we going to be okay waiting here for your brother? What if your colleagues come back?"

"Trust me, they'll be busy. After they see the devastation at the sheriff's department, they'll speak to her, find out that Ted's body was recovered, and they'll swing by the safe house to see it firsthand. Then their last stop will be the morgue. To bring Ted's body back to San Diego. There'll be lots of paperwork and it'll take hours."

"Okay. What do we do while we wait for your brother?"

He pointed to the only restaurant in the small airport and headed over.

The hostess greeted them with a smile and menus the size of poster boards.

"Booth, please," Nick said. "Can we get that one?" He pointed out one in the far rear, close to the kitchen, where the lighting was dimmer and no one else was seated. It'd also give him clear lines of sight to the front door and restrooms. If anything was coming for them, he'd know.

He flashed a wheedling smile instead of his badge.

"Sure," the hostess said and led them to the table he'd requested.

Nick ushered Lori with his palm at the small of her back, thought twice about the unnecessary contact and dropped his hand.

They sat across from each other with his back to the wall. A quick perusal of the menu showed him breakfast and lunch were both available until three.

A waitress came over and set two waters down. "Are you ready to order?"

"We have ten bucks and we're starving," Nick said. "What do you recommend?"

"Are you sharing?" the waitress asked.

"Yes," they said in unison.

Old habits die hard. Whenever they ordered takeout at the safe house, he and Lori always shared. It'd started with wanting to try the other's dish and morphed into standard practice.

"Then I suggest either the cheeseburger or the Reuben with fries."

"Reuben," he said.

At the same time, she said, "Cheeseburger."

Nick bit back a grin. "I know Reubens are your favorite."

"And I know you love to try the cheeseburgers at a new place," she said.

Why did she have to make it so hard to hate her and so easy to love her? "The Reuben, and feel free to be generous with the fries." He smiled and winked at her. "Pretty please." It wasn't often that he whipped out his charm card and played it, but he was starving and could wolf down an entire plate of fries on his own.

The simpering waitress nodded and withdrew.

He leaned back, folding his arms and looked at Lori. No smile. No wink.

If she thought that she could ambush him with a kiss—granted, it had been a full-scale bombardment on his senses, the definition of shock and awe—and sharing a meal was going to change his perspective, then she was sadly mistaken.

She wrung her hands and bit her lower lip like she was gearing up to say things he'd rather not hear. "I owe you an explanation."

"You don't owe me anything. There's nothing between us besides my sworn obligation as a US deputy marshal to protect a witness."

"Stop it," she said in a harsh whisper. "I may not have told you everything, but I have never lied to you. Please, don't start pretending like there's nothing between us. It's not fair to either of us."

"Fair?" He leaned forward, putting his arms on the table. "I admitted how I felt about you two hours ago. You told me it didn't matter. So why are you so hellbent on explaining anything?"

She took a deep breath, looking as rattled as he'd

felt after that insurgent-attack kiss. "Because you deserve to know."

That he found difficult to argue with. He didn't invest his heart lightly. And a piece of his belonged to Lori. He did deserve to know. "I'm listening."

Chapter Fourteen

Lori dug deep, trying to tap that wellspring of courage hidden somewhere inside her. "Things weren't quite as Belladonna had portrayed them. The divorce from my ex took a long time. Two years. While we were separated, hashing everything out, I met Dante Vargas at a company party. I knew he represented our biggest client, but I didn't know anything illicit was happening then. He was a little older. Very charming and debonair at first." Probably in the same manner Satan had been when he tempted Eve with the apple.

Nick squirmed, his face pinching with a sour look.

"Do you remember the things I told you about my dad?"

He nodded. "How he beat your mother and verbally abused you, called you worthless. The names he called you." His mouth flattened and his hands balled to fists.

"After I found out that my ex-husband was cheating on me, with so many different women in the office, and I confronted him, he told me it was my fault. For not being good enough. Not being better. That I should dress more provocatively like this one… Or not fight back, when he'd force himself on me."

Tears stung her eyes, but she had to reel them in,

stuff the sadness and pain and grief down. She didn't want Nick thinking that she was trying to manipulate him by crying. Some women did that. Lori wasn't one of them.

"I didn't know." His voice was brittle. "That he raped you."

Her heart throbbed in her chest. "Took a long time for me to even see it as rape. I mean, he was my husband. Right?"

"No, Lori." He reached for her hand.

But she pulled back. She wasn't telling him to get sympathy, only to help him understand her choices.

"Dante came into my life at my lowest point. He said all the right things. Swept me off my feet with lavish gifts and trips. That part is true. Here was this businessman who made me feel desirable and special. But it was all a facade."

God, she'd been so stupid, so blind to the truth. As ignorant as Eve.

"Didn't you suspect that his business wasn't legitimate?"

"No. A lot of our wealthy clients had personal security, the same as him. There were never any drugs around, no violence. He took his phone calls in private and I was never in his office."

The waitress brought the food to the table. She set the Reuben in front of Lori and a cheeseburger in front of Nick. "The cook made an extra by accident." She winked and strutted off.

Her appetite was gone. Nick must've lost his, as well, because he pushed his plate to the side.

"How did you get the new position?"

"It was Dante's idea. He said that the accountant handling their portfolio was retiring. Short notice. Looking back, I think he meant that the accountant was *being retired*." With a bullet to the back of the head. She swallowed down the bile rising in her throat. "I told him that with the messy divorce, I didn't want to rock the boat. He told me he would take care of it. Then my ex said that the promotion would be a part of the divorce settlement along with a lump sum of alimony five times the amount that he'd initially specified."

"How much?"

"Two million dollars. When I asked him why, he said it was for my pain and suffering."

"Why did you stay with WCM after you found out about his affairs?"

"I had a good position I enjoyed, but my in-laws convinced me. They said I was still family and that I'd always have a job there."

He nodded like he got that part. "And you found out about the money laundering once you started the new job."

"The weekend before I took over the new position, Dante insisted on moving me in with him. It felt rushed, too fast, but he's the type of person who is so persistent you can't say no to him." Her gut clenched thinking back on it. "It wasn't until we started living together, day in and day out, that I saw he didn't have relationships with people. To him, I wasn't a girlfriend. I was a possession. A piece of property. And the only reason he moved me in to begin with—"

"Was to watch you," he said, finishing her sentence, and she nodded. "Did you confront him about the money laundering?"

She shook her head. "No one confronts Dante. I

broached the subject." Dante wouldn't even discuss it until he'd stripped her naked and ensured she wasn't wearing a wire. That conversation had made her top five of all-time most humiliating. "He made it clear the money from my divorce settlement came from him and it was to keep quiet. Then he warned me never to discuss it again. So I didn't."

Nick's eyes narrowed. "Warned you how? Threatened you? With a gun? Knife?"

How could she explain it? "Dante is evil and insidious. He's like cancer. He didn't need a gun or a knife. Not with someone like me, anyway. You say the big C. Stage four. I get it. No explanation necessary."

"Did you keep sleeping with him?"

"I was in a different trap. Playing a different role. Acting in my own life. None of it was real. None of it brought me happiness. Not like what I found in spending time with you."

He looked away from her. "You call it spending time. I call it WITSEC. A part of my job."

She put her hand on his forearm. "Was kissing me part of your job, too?"

"No, but it was a mistake." He pulled his arm back and straightened. "How long did you launder their dirty money? How long did you let him touch you after you knew the truth?"

The heat of shame and embarrassment crawled up her face. "Six months," she said, low, the two words sour on her tongue.

His mouth twisted in disgust and she saw it again. The loathing in his eyes.

Her skin crawled remembering those six months with Dante the devil. The tense meals with her head in a guillotine, the awkward kisses that tasted of fear, forcing herself to detach as they had sex like she was having an out-of-body experience while her soul screamed for her to get away. Six months of dread ballooning in her chest, trying not to lose her mind, or her life.

"I needed time to come up with an exit strategy," she said, desperate to explain, for it to make sense to him, "and figure out how to pull it off."

The quiet air between them was weighted. She felt his gaze on her, his judgment, when she yearned for his understanding.

"Too bad you can't take all of that money with you into your new life." The more Nick said, the deeper Lori felt the cut.

She shook her head, her heart bleeding.

Where was her Nick? The one who could be gentle, comforting, compassionate?

"I never wanted their blood money," she said. "I gave it away. As soon as I found out it had come from Dante, I wrote a check to the Helping Hands Foundation." Her favorite charity that had kept the darkness from swallowing her when she was a teen. "They needed it. Not me."

The fact seemed to sober him, but it didn't soften him. "When I'm in the presence of evil, I sense it. Like an icy finger moving over my spine. How come you didn't feel it, that Dante Vargas, the biggest drug lord on the western seaboard, was evil?"

She'd asked herself the same question every single day for the past year. Dissecting her choices, analyzing her mistakes, so she didn't repeat them.

But Lori didn't think there was any answer that she could give that would satisfy Nick.

Two HOURS LATER, Nick and Lori were still picking at their food, content not to force the conversation further.

He kept turning it all over in his head.

Lori wasn't like ninety-five percent of the people who entered the WITSEC program—bottom-feeders. She was trying to get herself out of a bad situation and to survive. But how she'd gotten into that situation with Vargas to begin with niggled at him.

Had a part of her been tempted by his money and his power? Her ex-husband had been the same, but with Vargas, she'd gone from bad to worse. A cartel boss, a reputed psychopath.

As much as it unsettled him, he couldn't dismiss all the good things about her, either. She was the best thing to happen to him, even with *Los Chacales* on their asses. And he had never desired any woman the way he hungered for Lori.

He yearned to kiss her again, hold her, have her body molding to his—

But his brain kept spiraling back and snagging on Vargas.

"Hello there." Bo slipped into the booth beside him, catching him in a headlock and ruffling his hair. "I didn't expect to find you two moping and wearing matching his and hers outfits."

Damn it. How had Nick let his older brother get the drop on him? He'd never hear the end of it.

Nick wrangled his head loose. "Get off."

"You're slipping. No wonder you had to call me for help." Bo turned to Lori and extended his hand. "Bowen at your service, ma'am. Have no fear, the smarter, stealthier, more charming McKenna is here."

Nick rolled his eyes.

"Wow. That rhymed." She shook his hand. "I'm Lori. Nice to meet you."

"Listen, there is serious stuff going on," Nick snapped. "We need to stop shooting the breeze and get out of Dodge. Plenty of time to talk at home."

AIDEN STOOD, STARING at the charred remains of the Big Bear safe house. "What do you think of everything the sheriff said?"

Charlie shrugged. "It's hard to say. Nick is taking a big leap by accusing Draper of being the leak without any proof. And he is a hothead."

Aiden nodded. "And impulsive."

"And stubborn."

"But he's never been *unhinged*."

A one-shoulder shrug from Charlie. "It's not for us to reason why."

"It's for us to keep witnesses alive," Aiden said, finishing her sentence.

"As long as Hummingbird is still breathing and Nick gets her to the office tomorrow, so we can escort her to court on time, I don't think we should worry about the rest. For now."

"Agreed." Aiden's phone rang. He knew who it was before he answered. "Hello, sir."

"Did you find McKenna and Hummingbird?"

"Negative, sir. Both birds appear to have flown the coop."

Draper swore into the phone. "Who the hell does he think he is? Going dark! What is he thinking?"

He's probably thinking about keeping a witness alive.

"I'm not a mind reader, sir." He exchanged a knowing look with Charlie.

"He's endangering a witness. If anything happens to Hummingbird, it's McKenna's fault. Do you understand?"

Aiden let out a low sigh that wouldn't telegraph over the line. "Zeeman's body was found in the safe house."

"Go to the morgue. Bring his remains home with you. If you have any trouble, give me a call and I'll take care of it."

"Roger."

To be summoned was never good.

Dante Vargas had summoned Belladonna.

The director of the cartel's west coast branch—made him sound like he was a civilized banker instead of a psychotic drug-lord butcher—had packed up his entourage, driven two hours from San Diego to Laguna Beach, and set up shop in three adjacent oceanfront villas at the five-star Montage.

All to receive face-to-face confirmation as soon as possible that Lori Carpenter would no longer be a problem.

Belladonna had failed to deliver, and Dante wasn't happy.

Smokey pulled up in front of the center villa. "Should I wait for you?"

Translation: *Are you walking back out alive or being carried out wrapped in plastic?*

"Wait for me." She was walking back out, even if it meant she had to kill Dante to leave.

Belladonna opened her door and slid out gracefully,

wearing a white silk suit she'd changed into. A guard let her inside.

The first thing to greet her was a breathtaking, panoramic view of the ocean.

The second was a squad of armed men. She counted a baker's dozen.

Dante had obviously anticipated her enthusiasm to keep breathing.

Well, good on him.

Belladonna smiled, aware of the unnatural pull in her cheeks that contradicted the tension surging in her veins. She sauntered deeper into the foyer, her three-inch heels clickety-clacking across the marble floor. The place epitomized relaxed class and stellar beauty. Always nothing but the finest for Dante.

Rapid-fire, she formed an exit strategy.

That was her gift. To assess. To forecast.

Unfortunately, all scenarios she visualized left her wounded. The vast majority mortally, considering she only had one concealed weapon on her. But if she counted her right and left shoe heel each as deadly instruments, that'd give her three.

No matter how many times they patted her down, they never found the third.

Men.

But none of those weapons were as effective as a bullet. She was outmanned, outgunned, but not outsmarted. She'd have to talk her way out of this.

Belladonna raised her hands and assumed the position.

Beefcake Number One patted her down, copping a generous feel of her breasts, butt and had the gall to leer in her face when he cupped her sex.

Compartmentalizing, she stuffed her fury in a box and tucked it in her mental closet right beside a beautiful pair of Louboutins to offset the ugliness.

Then she thought about her innocent daughter, Lily, growing up and one day facing such humiliating treatment from some man who sought to bully and intimidate her.

To hell with that.

Belladonna punched him in the throat and slammed the heel of her palm up into his nose, breaking it with a delicious crunch.

Watching him crumple to his knees, gagging and bleeding, turned her smile from artificial to genuine in a snap.

The others surrounded her, semiautomatic HK MP5s at the ready in their meaty grasps.

She extended her bloody palm. "A napkin. I can't go in there looking a mess." Thankfully, she didn't seem to have any blood on her pristine white suit.

Dante was a stickler about appearances.

Beefcake Two ran and grabbed a napkin for her. She wiped off her hand and tossed it back at him.

"Señor Vargas wants you to remove your shoes," he said. "Please."

This shouldn't have surprised her—Dante had taken over as her mentor and commander when his father passed—but it did.

She slipped off the deadly, stainless-steel spike heels.

The marble floor was cold beneath her bare feet. She welcomed the sensation, hoping it would cool her temper, too.

Beefcake Two escorted her through the villa to the living room.

Dante sat on the sofa, legs crossed, an arm stretched across the back of the couch, sipping a drink. The tall glass was filled with ice, a pale liquid and mottled mint. She assumed it was a mojito.

For a man in his midfifties, time had worked in his favor. Like a fine wine, he aged well. He possessed the fit physique of a man in his prime. From a distance, he oozed sex appeal and charm and had this mesmerizing way of hooking you. But the closer you got to him, the easier it was to see the illusion. It was plain to see how the wolf had fooled the sheep, Lori Carpenter.

"Would you care for a beverage?" Dante asked.

"No, thank you." She kept her expression soft and her voice polite. "I'm working."

"Come now. I won't offer you a last meal. But surely I can give you a last beverage."

She scanned the floor for a polyurethane tarp. A telltale sign he planned to put a bullet in her head. There was none.

"I insist." Dante smiled with all the sweetness of battery acid. "What will you have?"

"Calvados," Belladonna said, brightly.

Dante pointed his finger at her and chuffed out a laugh devoid of humor. "Cheater." He wagged his finger.

Champagne, single malt scotch, rum, vodka, gin, bourbon and beer, Dante traveled with. He only had Calvados on hand at his home, but never had the apple brandy on the road. And it wasn't something he could simply send a goon to the local liquor store to fetch.

She shrugged, mustering her most charming smile. If she had to beg, steal, cheat or lie to get back to her family, then she would.

Before she met her husband, Alessandro, her life had been full—of violence and bloodshed—and she'd been fine. Perfectly fine. Then he drifted into her orbit. More like crashed and there was no stopping the collision. She became painfully aware of the emptiness inside, of how he made her ache to be better.

Only fools fell in love, but she'd fallen anyway.

Only those who got out of this bloody business—free and clear—were safe to saddle themselves with a defenseless child. But there was no *out*. Not for people like her.

And she'd had a kid anyway.

She was still fine, better than before, but if she lost them, or if they lost her…

What had she been thinking? No one could have it all and it had been greedy of her to try. But once you experienced the warm intoxication of love, tasted happiness, it changed everything.

So yes, she stood in front of Dante Vargas, trying to cheat death.

"Why isn't that bitch dead?" His smile evaporated.

"Nick McKenna has proven to be more formidable and resourceful than expected."

"But that is why I brought you in, Bella," he said, making her skin crawl. "You foresee and adapt."

"It's not over. I still have time to eliminate her."

"You've lost lots of rooks and bishops, but I don't see a scratch on my strongest piece. I don't think my king has seen much action, gotten up close and personal with this Nick McKenna. Why have you been playing it safe?"

Getting up close and personal on other jobs hadn't

scared her. If she had died back then, it wouldn't have mattered. But now…

The faces of Alessandro and Lily floated up in her mind's eye. Now she had two miraculous reasons to live.

"I have a contingency plan," she said with genuine confidence. "But I'll need more men."

The USMS was nothing if not predictable. McKenna might be rogue, playing it his way, but Marshal Draper would bring him back in line.

Dante picked up a remote control from the coffee table in front of him and turned on the TV that hung above the lit fireplace.

A video came on. Of her husband, playing with their daughter.

Dante knew about them. Knew where they were and was making a point that he could reach out and touch them. At any time.

Her heart withered and the taste of ash saturated her mouth.

"Your daughter is beautiful. She looks so happy. Carefree. I want her to stay that way. And your husband. Handsome, but I never would have imagined that you would've fallen for a college professor. Biology, no less."

And that was when the game flipped, and hope sparked anew.

Her husband's cover was intact.

Dante had no clue that Alessandro was deadlier than she was. That meant only one man had been sent to keep an eye on them, two at the most, since there was no perceived threat.

She looked back at the video, playing on a loop.

Their daughter wore the garish two-piece she'd regretted buying, the one Alessandro hated with a passion. Seeing Lily run across the beach wearing it was a message.

Alessandro was aware they were under surveillance and he had it under control. She would've taken a relieved breath if not for the fear that Dante would've registered it.

"Please, don't hurt them," she said as if reading from a script. Alessandro would rip out the carotid artery of anyone who got close to their daughter.

"Believe me, that is not what I want." Dante stood and walked up to her. He grasped her chin between his thumb and forefinger and tipped it up. *"Belleza deslumbrante."*

Ravishing beauty.

It made her want to puke.

"Why should I give you another chance?" Dante asked. "Why should I let your family live?"

Fury bubbled inside her, but she masked it with a sly grin. "Because I brought you a gift."

Dante released her and stepped back. Way, way back like he was afraid.

After threatening her family, he should be.

"Unless it's Lori Carpenter's head in a box, I'm not sure I want it," he spat.

She considered going for her concealed weapon, the hairpin that secured her bun in place. It was as lethal as an ice pick. She'd have time to cross the room and stab him in the jugular before his guards entered. But then she would be stuck.

"Trust me, you'll want it." Belladonna raised her palms.

His shoulders relaxed at the conciliatory gesture.

Slowly, she reached inside her silk camisole, into

her bra, and retrieved the USB drive tucked under her breast. She was a generous C cup. Between the ample padding in her push-up bra and her fleshy tissue, the guard never would've felt it.

Belladonna offered him the drive in her palm.

"What is it?" he asked, taking cautious steps, closing the distance between them.

"The California WITSEC list and the name of every deputy marshal in the Golden State."

Dante beamed. That was right; she was walking out of there.

"How did you get this?" he asked, taking the drive.

That was for her to know and for him never to find out. "It's like you said. I foresee and adapt."

He cupped her cheek and lifted her face, bringing her lips to his, and kissed her. Closed mouth, but nonetheless revolting.

Her stomach cramped and she wished she'd worn her poisoned lipstick.

"There is no one else in the world like you, Belladonna." He kept his face close, the stench of rum brushing over her skin.

She couldn't wait to take a shower.

"Kill Lori Carpenter and I will let you go."

Her heart leaped, but her mind spun like a pinwheel. "What?"

"Kill her for me and I'll set you free. You can go and live your life with your family without looking over your shoulder."

He is the prince of lies, a maestro of manipulation.

But what if he meant it? What if she could be free?

"I want that bitch dead before she testifies. Fail me, I'll make you watch as I skin your husband alive, and then I'll kill you and take your daughter. Train her to be your replacement. The same way my father took you when yours failed him. I have a lovely name already picked out for her. I shall call her...Oleander."

Chapter Fifteen

The storm stalked them from California to Nevada, thunderclouds darkening the early-evening sky. No rain yet, but it would come.

As the bright lights of his family's compound came into view, a sense of peace washed over Nick. The mountains rose up behind the property set on five acres, and to the east was a partial view of the Vegas strip in the distance.

There was no safer place on earth for Lori. He'd imagined bringing her here during his conversations with his mother. What it would be like having her in his childhood home, surrounded by people who knew him best. Sharing the other side of himself with her.

But none of his delusions had been under such horrible circumstances. It was the dose of reality he needed.

The drone of the helicopter's engine had smothered his anger and quieted his mind on the ride. If he thought of Lori only as a witness, then it was possible to keep his emotions in check and his perspective objective. So that was what he decided to do.

Bo landed on the helipad and shut the chopper down. As the rotor blades slowed, Nick took Lori's hand and helped her climb out. The small touch sent electricity firing across his nerves, wreaking havoc on his brain.

As long as he didn't touch her, he might be able to think of her as only a witness.

Nick broke the physical contact between them, and the striking loss of heat was immediate. She drew in a sharp breath, her shadowed gaze capturing his, and wet her lips.

Had she felt it, too, that spark of connection?

His pulse pounded in his veins for reasons that had nothing to do with danger.

He paused to take in the sight of her set against the backdrop of his family home. Those doe eyes, her fine-boned features, that pale, rose-colored mouth he longed to kiss until they were both breathless. Even though they were outside, the space around him seemed to shrink, condensing to her. She was everything he'd always desired, and he wanted her.

Not only to have her in his bed and appease this craving that was as terrific as it was terrible, but also he wanted her to be his, to hold and protect and love.

Maybe he was fooling himself to think objectivity with Lori was possible, or maybe loving her made him a fool.

He wished he could tell the difference. The one thing there was no denying—he wasn't just crazy about Lori Carpenter. He loved her.

It was the only explanation for his jealousy over Vargas and why her past grated on him.

Coming up alongside them, Bo whistled. "So you're the hottie my brother is sweet on."

Nick squirmed on the inside but didn't dare let Bo see it. "I never called you that. Not that you're not attractive." Lori was a knockout, but it wasn't her beauty that had stolen his heart.

The ache in his chest returned at the thought of her with Vargas. He wanted to strangle the man.

Lori blushed, her gaze lowering.

"In his defense," Bo said, "he never referred to you as a *hottie* to our mother."

Her eyes and her brows lifted. "You talked to your mother about me?"

Nick elbowed his brother in the ribs to keep his mouth shut. "I may have mentioned you in vague terms, once or twice."

Bo laughed. "Yeah, once or twice. Anyway, Nick only falls for hotties. So we all assumed."

"Your family has talked about me?" Lori asked, wrapping her arms around herself.

"Once or twice. Come on," Bo said, spurring them to walk to the house. "The moment I told Mom that you were bringing your witness here, she went to the kitchen and started cooking. I'm sure she's got a feast waiting inside. Hope you're both hungry."

"I'm starving," Lori said.

Nick's appetite had also returned with a vengeance.

"Good," Bo said. "Because not eating would offend her."

They ascended the front steps to the wide wrap-around porch.

Bo marched inside with his usual bravado. "They're here!"

Nick ushered Lori inside ahead of him and closed the door. The large house smelled of turmeric and corian-der and saffron. Scents he equated with safety and love.

Whenever he came back home, after he'd decided

to carve his own path separate from his family, it was always strange but comforting at the same time. Like putting on your favorite pair of worn-in shoes that no longer fit.

Speaking of which, he pulled off his still-wet shoes and socks and put them in the row of other footwear by the door. Bo did the same and Lori followed suit.

His mother, Pamela Maadi-McKenna, drifted into the foyer barefoot, wearing a long kaftan in a dramatic print of jewel colors, mostly sapphire and emerald, her jet-black hair in a messy-chic top knot. She always made flawless perfection look effortless.

Lori did, as well. She didn't have to try. Sans makeup, windswept hair, sweats that hugged her lean, curvy frame, she was absolutely stunning.

His mother wrapped him in a tight hug, then kissed his cheeks three times. She bracketed his face with her palms and looked at him as if she hadn't seen him in years.

"You did right to come home," his mother said, by-passing pleasantries and lightening his heavy spirit with the very first words from her mouth.

Mom swung her bright-eyed attention to Lori like Nick was now yesterday's news. "Welcome." She clutched Lori's arms and kissed her cheeks. "I'm Pam."

"Lori. Nick talks about his family all the time with such great affection. It's a pleasure to meet you. Thank you for allowing me to come. I'm sorry to put you through all this trouble."

"It's no trouble." Mom took Lori's hand and held it between both of hers.

Lori threw him a questioning glance. He hadn't

thought to explain his mother's peculiar ways before they had entered the house.

Flashing a shallow grin, he shrugged.

His mother stood there, smiling at Lori, holding her hand, doing her *thing* that made newcomers uneasy at the five-second mark based on the comments and questions that came afterward.

Explaining why his mother held someone's hand while staring at them in silence didn't help. In fact, it tended to push the awkward meter closer to unsettling. Girlfriends declined to come back to the house. Not that he'd brought anyone home in nearly a decade.

Pamela Maadi-McKenna had a gift. He wasn't sure what to call it. His father had said she had a sixth sense. Could touch a person and tell things about them.

She shook my hand, stared in my eyes for ten seconds, his dad had said, *and told me that she didn't mean to scare me, but that I was the love of her life, that we were going to get married on a beautiful spring day, have three children and be happy. I thought she was a sandwich short of a picnic at the time, but she was so gosh-darn gorgeous and confident. Instead of running for the hills, I asked her out on a date, and it was the best decision of my life. Always listen to your mother, boy.*

Nick clasped his mother's shoulder and gave a squeeze that signaled *please stop*. "Whatever you cooked smells delicious."

"Yes, yes," his mother said, taking the hint and releasing Lori's hand. She gave his cheek a pat. "Show Lori to the bathroom so she can freshen up and we'll eat." His mother drifted off to the kitchen.

Nick guided Lori down the hall. "I'm sorry about my mom."

"Sorry about what?"

"Her holding your hand and staring at you. I promise she's not crazy."

"I didn't mind. I liked it. A very warm, intimate way to greet someone."

It was intimate all right, bordering on invasive, but it pleased him that she felt welcomed because he knew that she would be. He stopped in front of the bathroom. "Take your time. Mom keeps basic toiletries in the cabinet. The dining room is through there." He pointed to his right. "You can't miss it."

"Thanks. I'll only be a minute." She held his gaze a moment, and he wanted to say more but couldn't find the right words. Then she closed the door.

He went the way he'd indicated and found Bo talking to his sister Julie.

"Hey, Jules." Nick hugged his little sister, relaxing a little more. "I wasn't sure if you'd be in or out skip tracing."

"Just finished an hour ago. We had a guy jump bail, but when I heard your mysterious witness that you've been safeguarding for a year was coming, I couldn't miss the chance to meet her. Kicked down the right doors, knocked around the right heads and found him. So where is she?" Jules's eyes danced like those of a giddy teenager.

"Bathroom." Nick figured it was best to address the elephant in the room before it turned and stampeded him. "Look, I don't know what Mom told you guys, but Lori is not my girlfriend. She's just a witness. Let's keep it professional."

Jules winked. "Right, sure. *Professional.*" Her gaze lifted somewhere behind him and by the gigantic grin spreading on his sister's face, he guessed Lori had entered the room. "Hi, I'm Julie," she said, shoving him to the side, "but everyone calls me Jules. It's so nice to meet you."

Jules hugged Lori and thankfully gave her room to breathe.

"I'm Lori. It's nice to meet you, as well."

His mom came in and set platters down on the set table. "Let's eat. Lori, please." She gestured to a seat beside her.

Everyone sat. His mother outdid herself preparing all his favorites. Kabobs, *fesenjoon*, *kashke bademjan*— eggplant dip—tamarind-stuffed fish, saffron rice, *dolmeh*, stuffed grape leaves, and yogurt cucumber sauce with rose petals.

"This spread is incredible," Lori said.

"Thank you." His mother encouraged her to help herself.

The table hung in quiet anticipation waiting for Lori to taste the food.

"Oh, my God. This is beyond delicious, Mrs. McKenna. I can see where Nick gets his love of food. I wish I'd had this growing up."

"Call me Pam, please. I'm happy you like it."

"Love it." Lori practically had a food orgasm with each bite.

Nick couldn't help but wonder what face she'd make with him buried deep inside her, writhing in pleasure as he brought her to the brink and pulled her back before letting her orgasm.

Lowering his gaze, he shook the wicked thought from his head.

"Red wine?" his mom offered, and when Lori nodded, she filled her glass and passed the bottle.

"I have to tell you what an amazing son you've raised," Lori said between bites. "I owe him my life. He's the bravest, most honest man I've ever met and is kind enough to share his food with me. Doesn't get much better than that." She turned her sparkling gaze to him, and he wished the circumstances, all around, had been different.

"Keeping you alive is my job," Nick said, his tone harsher than he'd intended.

"But sharing your food with me wasn't. Or your mom's recipes."

"Really?" his mom asked. "Nick never seems interested in cooking here at home."

"We cooked all the time together. Three or four times a week. But I have to confess, the *fesenjoon* we made wasn't half as good."

His mother gave him a knowing look and smiled at his scowl. She liked Lori a lot. It was hard for anyone not to.

"So how's the bounty-hunting business going?" Nick asked, eager to change the subject.

"Good." Bo stuffed more food into his mouth.

"What else did you and Nick do together tucked away in a safe house for a year?" Jules waggled her eyebrows.

"We talked a lot, went jogging, played board games, watched movies, but cooking was the best."

It had been the best. That was when they swapped childhood stories. Hers had been dark and his had been complicated, but happy. It was the most sharing he'd ever done in any relationship.

"What was Nick like as a kid? Saint or hellion?"

Glances passed between his family members. "Hellion," they all said together.

Nick grimaced. "Lori doesn't want to hear about that."

"But I do." Her eyes shone with curiosity.

"Well then, I don't want to hear about it," Nick snapped. "Okay?"

Blessed silence.

Everyone ate and Nick hoped no one spoke another word during the entire meal.

Of course, it only took two minutes before his mother said, "Lori, what do you do?"

"I'm an—"

"She can't talk about it," Nick interrupted, and his mother responded with a glare of daggers.

"You all have your mom's coloring and soulful eyes," Lori said. "I've seen pictures of your dad, and I can see the resemblance in the boys, but Jules, you're a spitting image of your mom. So beautiful."

"Thank you!" Jules sat a little taller in her chair. "I love you already. I can see what Nick sees in you."

"So can I," his mother said.

Did his mom mean that in the way a regular person would, or had she *seen* something?

He'd learned long ago it was best not to wonder and certainly not to ask.

Forks finally lowered to the plates as the last of the wine was poured.

"Nicky," his mother said. "Help me in the kitchen with dessert."

They cleared the table of the platters of food and plates.

Carrying the nine-inch hand-painted gilded plates that had been set out, he joined his mother at the counter in front of his favorite dessert. The most delicious thing in the world. A three-layered chocolate cake with ganache and mascarpone pistachio filling.

She only made it on his birthday. A time for celebration. But he wasn't feeling festive.

"What is wrong with you? Why are you so cranky?" she asked.

"Cranky? What am I, a damn toddler?"

"Language."

"Sorry." He hung his head. "It's been a tough day. I've earned the right to be grumpy."

"You both look like you've been through hell. But I don't understand you. For a year you've talked to me about the woman sitting in the other room. Fifty-two conversations about all the things you admire and adore about her."

Nick shot his mother a *cranky* look. He'd never used the word *adore*. Even if he did on some level.

"You've never spoken about any woman with such affection. Not even that *girl* you married."

Nick winced. "Mom. Don't bring that up." They had only been twenty-one, both of them had been drunk and wrong for each other. It had only lasted twenty-seven days. The shortest marriage in McKenna or Maadi history.

"My point is, you're enamored," his mother said. "I dare go so far as to say in love with her. Yet, you are so cold and distant with Lori. Why?"

"You wouldn't understand."

She tapped him hard on the nose with two fingers. "Ouch!"

"Don't be such a baby," she said, slicing the cake. "And don't be condescending. I understand more than you think."

"I meant you wouldn't understand because you're not in the USMS and have never worked with a witness."

She cupped his cheek. "I may not be a marshal, but I am a mother." She returned to plating the cake.

He put his hand on her forearm before she cut a fifth piece. "We only need four. I'm not having any."

"You could use a little sweetness. Trust me on that." She cut a fifth slice anyway. "What is wrong, *azizam?*" his mother asked, calling him *my dear* in Farsi.

"I found out some things about Lori that I'm having difficulty with."

She clucked her tongue, plating the slices. "You're always so hard on everyone. Expecting people to meet some impossible standard of perfection that they can't live up to. And when they don't, you pull away and cut them off. It's almost as if you only want what you can't have and once you get it, you find fault. If you continue like this, you'll deny yourself happiness and live a lonely life."

He had put Lori on a pedestal and crowned her with a halo when she was human and fallible the same as him. Rather than showing her compassion when she was at her most vulnerable, baring her soul, he'd gifted her with anger and jealousy. Completely disregarded how she'd been manipulated and used.

Nick gritted his teeth, hating himself.

"I have sat with her, touched her, *read* her." His mother let that sink in. "Lori has a good heart. And it is

plain to see that she loves you. Have you ever done anything that you've regretted, that you were ashamed of?"

Horrible things. Things he'd shared with Lori and
she hadn't turned her back on him or judged him. She'd
shown him affection and acceptance instead. Love.

"I thought so," his mother said, wagging a finger.

"Did you read me? Is that how you know?" He stiffened, hoping she hadn't.

"No, *azizam*. I didn't have to. We've all done things
that we regret. That bring us some measure of shame.
The choices you two have made, the roads you've each
taken, have led you both here, together. It's okay to be
a fool for love, so long as you are not a damn fool."

The difference suddenly struck him, and he had his
answer. "Mom, *language*."

She dismissed him with a wave of her hand. "Help
me serve dessert."

They carried the cake into the dining room, where
Bo was pouring brandy and Lori was laughing with his
siblings. The sound of her joy warmed his heart.

He had all the people he cared about most in the
world in one room and somehow, he'd been too narrow
sighted to enjoy it.

"Nicky, why don't you and Lori eat outside?" his
mother said. "Enjoy the view and the fresh air."

LORI TOOK NICK'S nod to his mother's suggestion as a
hopeful sign. He'd been tense and terse during dinner.
The opposite of what she'd expected.

They strolled out onto the porch and sat side by side
on the patio sofa. Another hopeful sign. Watching the
storm roll in, lightning flickering in the distance, the
low rumble of thunder, the air heavy with the promise

of rain, they ate dessert and drank brandy together the way they had so many times at the safe house without the alcohol.

Tomorrow she'd testify, and they'd go their separate ways. She didn't know if she'd have an opportunity to tell him all the things in her heart after she took the stand, much less in private. This was her chance and she was going to take it. "Nick, you're the first real thing in my life. Our friendship. What I feel for you. The happiness, the safety, the…love. It's all real for me."

He set his plate and brandy glass down. "I think I know why you fell for your husband and didn't see that Dante was evil."

She braced for some harsh retort, her stomach muscles clenching. All the men in her life had disappointed her, ultimately objectifying her and not seeing her as good enough. To receive the same rejection from Nick, in his home, surrounded by his caring family, might be more than she could handle.

But he took her hand in his, brushing his fingers across her knuckles, like they were a couple, bound together by more than his job. "They were abusers, like your dad. Their tactics were subtle and insidious at first. That's why you didn't see it. I know Vargas is a psychotic scumbag because I'm trained to see it. It's my job to know, but it wasn't yours."

"A part of me realizes that I was set up and manipulated. But another part feels like I should've seen it coming. Or to solely blame my ex-husband and Dante is shirking responsibility."

"The vast majority of people are happy to shirk responsibility for their mistakes and problems. Not you. But you're not at fault for what they did to you and I shouldn't have gotten so bent out of shape over Vargas. I was jealous."

If only he knew how little there was for him to be jealous of. "I'm sorry for not confiding in you sooner."

An odd vulnerability softened his eyes. "No, I'm the one who's sorry. For disappointing you when you finally tried to explain. You needed me to listen, to be the best version of myself, and instead I gave you Deputy Marshal Dredd."

She snickered, loving him even more for owning up to it.

"Our pasts have made us who we are. It's what brought us together. To get sidetracked by anything else is foolish. You're the best thing that's ever happened to me, knowing you, falling in love with you. No matter what happens tomorrow or the day after, I need you to know that this is real."

"I don't want to think about tomorrow. Only about right now. Spend the night with me." Her request dangled between them, leaving her feeling exposed.

His eyes gleamed in the moonlight. Lori held her breath, waiting for his response.

He gave a sultry smile that stirred butterflies to take flight in her belly.

Pam came out onto the porch. "I know it's been a long, exhausting day for you both. I've made up the bed in your room for Lori. Jules set out some things for you that should fit. Nicky, you can stay in the spare bedroom in the basement."

"If it's okay with Lori and you, Mom, I'd prefer to be upstairs in my room."

Lori smiled, her cheeks turning pink. "I'd prefer that, too."

His mother folded her arms. "I don't know about that."

"I'm not supposed to let her out of my sight," Nick said, his tone matter-of-fact. "No funny business."

"No. Funny. Business." She wagged a finger. "Come in before it starts raining." His mother picked up their dirty dishes and went back inside.

He waited a beat or two and said, "I'm going to make love to you. And if I do anything that remotely comes across as funny, then I'm doing it wrong."

Lori laughed.

Cupping the back of her head, he leaned in, closed his mouth over hers in a long, lingering kiss. "Tonight I want to erase the past, everything that came before us."

An exorcism of the darkness and a possession of something beautiful. She wanted that, too, for it to be carnal pleasure and sacred communion.

"Take me to bed," she whispered across his lips, "but I have no intention of us getting any sleep."

"Good. Neither do I."

Hand in hand they entered the house. The aromatic delight from dinner was still rich in the air. Chatter came from the kitchen.

"Should we go say good-night?" she asked in a low voice.

He shook his head, giving her a sly grin, and led her upstairs.

The wall along the stairwell was filled with family pictures. Pam and his father on their wedding day, Nick with his siblings as children playing, their father teaching them how to shoot. Smiles, hugs, laughter and warmth radiated from each one. A wall of love.

Lori's heart squeezed and she tightened her fingers around Nick's.

At the top of the landing, she asked, "Where's your mom's room?"

"First floor." He gave her a quick, light kiss. "Wait here a sec."

Nick disappeared down the hall and crept into another room.

Lori turned to see more photos. Pam sat in a rocking chair; an older toddler stood beside her knees with his head in her lap, she held a baby in her arms and her belly was round with more life. There was a look of utter contentment on her face.

An ache blossomed in her chest. She thought about what it would be like to have Nick's baby in her belly, in her arms. She'd never felt safe enough to ever entertain the idea of motherhood. The danger still hadn't passed, yet if it did, this was what she wanted, children and a house full of warmth, with him.

Nick hurried back, carrying condoms, and whisked her into his room.

Before she had a chance to take in the bedroom he'd grown up in, he kicked the door shut and pulled her into his arms, his face coming down to press a kiss to her lips.

Butterflies swarmed in her belly, and her arms made their way around his neck, her fingers tangled in his thick, cool hair.

Their tongues met in an erotic slide. In the gentle cage of his arms, his hands, the pressure of his mouth, there was the sublime balance of tender roughness. His desire for her was unmistakable as well as his awareness of her comfort. He took care not to agitate her bruises while conveying the intensity of his passion.

Magic.

The smooth, slow licks of his tongue were deep and intoxicating, teasing her with the promise of what was to come. She could kiss him for hours, getting drunk on this foreplay alone. The desire for that, hours, days, a lifetime of his kisses, made her chest constrict.

He guided her to the bed in a sensual dance, their bodies swaying to music meant only for them, and lowered her down.

The evidence of his desire, the impressive thickness, nudged against her belly. Need for him pulsed between her legs.

Taking her face between his hands, he fused their mouths, pressing his tongue deep, unleashing her hunger for more intimate penetration.

When he pulled his lips away, she was left panting for breath and melting around him.

He peeled her clothing off, taking care with her injuries, and she helped him, eager to have every inch of herself exposed to his touch. "You're so beautiful. Not just your body, but your soul. I'm so lucky."

His words made her heart squeeze and soar at the same time.

As she stripped him, her fingers sifted through the dusting of hair on his chest, lingered on the ridges of his sculpted abs. Absorbed the heat of his bare skin. After months of flirting and wanting and craving, to finally have him was glorious.

Cupping her breasts, he took one nipple into his mouth and toyed with the other. Every wet tug of his mouth and sweep of his tongue drove her wild.

She clutched him tighter, pressed her belly to the thick, straining shaft between them, and rubbed her body against his with matching urgency.

It was like stoking a fire, and a maddening yearning took over. She was so aroused; she might die if she didn't have him inside her.

Taking his hips, she guided him to the cleft between her thighs. "I need you." She fumbled for a condom, ripped it open and rolled it down over his shaft.

"I wanted to get you there with my mouth first." He nibbled on her earlobe, and she tingled at the thought.

"How about we take each other there later? I need you inside me right now. I can't wait."

He slid his hand to the place that ached for him; his fingers tested her readiness and spread her open.

Anticipation was a white-hot rush in her veins. The blunt tip pushed at her core, breached it, stretched her. She clutched his firm ass and pulled him into her to the hilt. He was hot and thick, and the searing kiss he gave her was a claiming. Soul to soul.

It was ecstasy.

Each slick thrust, each passionate brush of his lips, healed something inside her. Showed her what it was like to make love. To be cherished.

Agonizing need coiled tight in her core. Her whole body went taut as whimpers spilled from her, eyes squeezing shut, her nails digging into his back. She fell to pieces in his arms, doing her best to be quiet. And failing.

Just before the last rippling aftershock, he followed her over the edge. One last thrust, he stiffened and collapsed on top of her.

He held her close—his fingers in her hair, her cheek

to his chest—and rolled them onto their sides, staying buried inside her.

For the first time in her life, she was completely connected to another, in every way possible. The closeness, this love, was everything she'd been missing but needed.

Chapter Sixteen

"I'll have Hummingbird there this morning," Nick said over a new burner phone he'd gotten from Bo.

"You better," Yaz said. "Not only will Draper have your ass if you don't, but he'd be justified."

"I'm not asking you to buy stock in what I've said about Draper, but the fact is we have been compromised. All I'm asking is that you tell him I'm bringing her in at ten-thirty by car. But I want you and Charlie to meet us at the helipad on the roof at ten." That way if Draper planned to sabotage her arrival, the misinformation would be enough to still protect Lori. "We'll bring her inside and you and the rest of the SOG unit that's coming in can make sure she gets to court safely."

The tactical team would be locked and loaded with an arsenal of firepower and prepared to handle absolutely anything on the one-minute drive from the US Marshals' office to the federal courthouse.

"The support unit is here. They got in last night."

"Good. I'm not asking you to stick your neck out. I'm just asking for help with the added precaution. I've kept her alive thus far. Help me get her through the homestretch."

"It's a small ask. We can make it happen."

"Thanks, Yaz."

"You realize the moment Hummingbird is in the building and Draper sets eyes on you, you're fired, right?"

"I figured as much. But I'm not going to stop digging until I find proof that the SOB is involved. And when I do, it's his funeral."

"I totally didn't just hear you threaten a US marshal."

Nick raked a hand back through his hair. "Thanks. See you in a few hours." He hung up.

Aiden and Charlie could be trusted, and it'd be easy to explain the small deviation in plans as a last-minute change. Bringing Lori to the district office first was part of their protocol that Nick agreed was in her best interest.

A full SOG unit would have personnel posted outside the courthouse, in front of the US Marshals' district office, and escort her across the street to the federal courthouse using ballistic protective shields to cover her as the vehicle entered the courthouse.

The procedure was solid. The only opportunity Draper would have to sabotage things was as Nick delivered her to the office. But he wasn't going to give him the chance.

Nick finished his breakfast and his coffee, setting the dishes in the kitchen sink. Lori was still getting ready upstairs and said she couldn't eat with her nerves kicking up.

"You don't look well rested," his mother said, making a fresh pot of coffee.

He wasn't. Blissfully exhausted and thoroughly content was more like it. He and Lori had made love through the storm and the rest of the night. If he'd been a gentleman, he would've let her get more sleep. But he had to release a year of pent-up longing and lust. Taking her in the shower, licking his way down her delicious body and feasting between her legs back in the bed.

Her appetite had matched his rapacity, only heightening his arousal. They'd consumed each other and once their need had been temporarily slaked, they'd spooned.

They managed to doze for all of two hours.

Nick grabbed another piece of bacon from a platter. "It was hard to sleep with the storm."

"The storm outside or inside?" his mother asked.

Nick averted his gaze and stuffed the bacon into his mouth.

"I trust there was no *funny* business."

"No, ma'am," he said in total honesty.

"Good." She shot him a knowing glance. "If there had been, you would've been doing it wrong."

Nick choked on the food sliding down his throat.

Bo walked into the kitchen from the dining room with his empty plate and patted him on the back. "Are you all right, Nicky?"

"Your brother has never been better." His mother flashed a wry smile. "Isn't that right?"

It was true. Better. Happier. Lighter. His heart was like a hot-air balloon taking flight in his chest. "I should go check on Lori."

"She'll be down when she's ready. Jules wanted to make sure Lori had an outfit for today that she'd be comfortable in."

As if they'd talked her up, Lori entered the room. Wearing one of his sister's practical dresses—since Jules wasn't a suit gal—a pair of his mom's heels and a stunning smile, Lori looked beautiful.

Her dark hair was fashioned in a style he'd never seen on her, swept up in a twist off her shoulders. It flattered her, highlighting her features, warm eyes, high cheekbones, those kissable lips. But he'd prefer to see it loose and spread across his pillow again.

Their gazes collided and stuck. His pulse quickened and his heart grew even lighter. It was all he could do not to whisk her into his arms, hold her close, tight, and kiss her.

They'd been perfect together, fit like they belonged. Not just physically. It'd been the most satisfying carnal experience but also the most intimate.

God, why had he denied himself, them both, this pleasure for so long? Why didn't he make love to her sooner?

"Excellent choice," his mother said. "You look ready to take on a titan."

Lori's brow wrinkled, and Nick could practically hear her thoughts. Did his mother know Lori was about to go up against Goliath, a titan?

Nick had no clue whether his mother knew. He appreciated their unspoken *don't ask, don't tell* family policy.

"Are you sure I can't fix you something to eat on the flight?" his mother asked.

"No, I'm fine. With the jitters, I won't be able to eat until after I've testified."

"Good luck, my dear." Hugs and kisses were exchanged. "Nicholas," his mother said, pressing a palm to his cheek, "it's not over. Stay vigilant. I fear the worst is yet to come."

If there was more his mother could've said to help him, she would've.

No MATTER HOW frightening, no matter how risky, there was only one thing she could do.

Belladonna checked the time again. 9:50 a.m. She didn't know when the target would arrive at the US Marshals' office, or how. In a car driven down Broadway, entering through the garage, or by helicopter on the roof.

But the marshals would follow protocol down to the letter, and the target would be brought to their headquarters and then escorted to the federal courthouse. A full Special Operation Group contingency team was on the ground and waiting. They'd be geared up in body armor, locked and loaded to blow away any threat.

Belladonna was counting on the SOG not to disappoint. Her plan depended on it.

She'd positioned the replacement pawns, bishops and rooks in their respective places at the crack of dawn while the city was still sleeping. Each had their role to play. Everyone was under strict orders not to deviate from the plan.

A gambit if ever there was one to be played.

The carnage would be devastating, splashed across the news headlines for days. Many lives would be lost. But the only ones she cared about were hers, Alessandro's and Lily's.

It'd be nice if Smokey made it, too.

She clenched the burner phone in her hand, her knuckles whitening. The text message would have to be perfectly timed. She patted the messenger bag in the passenger seat. Her ace in the hole. It would work. It had to.

Glancing at the back of her hand, she was pleased the body makeup covering the rose tattoo hadn't smudged.

Her gaze flickered up to the rearview mirror of the parked sedan she sat in. Her short blond wig looked natural. She almost believed the disguise herself.

"Helicopter inbound," Smokey said over her earpiece that was hidden by the wig. "Civilian. ETA two minutes."

"It's them. I need synchronized execution of the fireworks. Wait for my mark."

"We're ready. The next time you radio in, the entire team will be able to hear you."

Excellent.

She took out her burner cell and sent the text.

Time to trim the bonsai.

Within thirty seconds she received Alessandro's response to her code for him to neutralize any threats, take their daughter and run to their contingency location.

Clippers in hand. See you soon.

Belladonna removed the battery from the phone, snapped the SIM card and chucked everything out the window. If things went as she expected, then she would indeed see them soon.

She put the car in Drive and turned down Broadway.

Nick McKenna was playing hide-and-seek, oblivious to the real game. This was an Armageddon match and he was blind to her next move.

THE GREETING LORI received from Nick's teammates was hurried. She got the feeling they didn't want to have her exposed outside for too long. Besides catching their names, Aiden Yazzie and Charlie Killinger, the rest had been a blur as they hustled her inside and down to the third floor.

The reception from Will Draper had been even colder. He threw a scowl at Nick and cut his eyes to her. "Ms. Carpenter, it's good to see you again," Will Draper said to her, escorting her to his office without so much as a handshake. "I was under the impression you wouldn't arrive for another hour. By car." His sour expression deepened to a pointed glare he turned on Nick and his two teammates.

Nick closed the office door. "We had to change the plan at the last minute."

"Not one word out of you. You're an embarrassment to this office and you're fired. I want your badge, your gun and you out of my sight," Draper snapped in a rush as though he'd been holding the words in and couldn't keep them bottled up a second longer.

"Excuse me, Marshal Draper," Lori said, the anger firing in her veins spurring her to step forward. "But Nick McKenna deserves a decoration, not a reprimand. The only reason I'm alive is because of him. Considering how the breach in this office jeopardized my safety several times, and not your deputy's actions, I'm shocked you're not showing more gratitude to someone who has gone above and beyond the call of duty. If he's not part of my protective detail to the courthouse, then I won't be testifying today."

Draper's jaw dropped and his face turned beet red. "Ms. Carpenter, with all due respect, you aren't privy to our standard operating procedures and the various rules Deputy Marshal McKenna has broken."

"Marshal Draper, you weren't almost killed multiple times and on the run for your life over the last twenty-four hours. You don't know the first thing about what we endured or survived out there. If that man," she said, pointing to Nick, "isn't properly commended and promoted for his efforts, then you either have your head up your butt or he's right and you're a traitor to justice. And I want you to know that I intend to share my perspective not only with the US attorney's office but also with the attorney general and my congressman."

BELLADONNA PASSED THE front of the US Marshals' office, where deputies in full tactical gear stood out front. She drove up to the parking garage of the building and spoke to the armed security guard, flashing the star pinned to the outside of the black badge holder that hung around her neck. "Hi, I'm Deputy Marshal Sharon White down from the LA office. I have an appointment with Marshal Draper."

The security guard turned to his laptop, verified her appointment, and waved to two more SOG deputies kitted in armor from top to toe to let her through.

Belladonna's hacker had planted the fake appointment while in their system.

She entered the garage and picked the first available spot. Getting out of the car, she touched her earpiece. "Stay on your objective, no matter what, until I say Echo Sierra." The siege would end, and Smokey would do one last thing for her. "Begin in thirty."

Counting down in her head, she tapped the device once more so nothing else could be heard on her side.

Twenty-eight. She walked through the lot and entered the building.

Twenty. Her heart pounded hard against her ribs as she crossed the lobby to the reception desk, but she had nerves of steel.

Sixteen. She repeated the same thing she'd told the guard outside, all the while keeping the count in her head.

Eleven. The man seated behind the desk eyed the badge prominently displayed and waved her through to security to have her bag checked.

Eight. Belladonna sat the messenger bag on the security table and flashed a smile. Nothing sexy, no teeth showing—a casual *hey, how are you* grin.

Five. Opening the main compartment, the armed guard returned the smile. *Four.* He took out the laptop, looked it over, noting the US Marshal Services label—*three*—and slid it back inside. *Two.* Then he turned the bag over and reached for the zipper of the back compartment.

One.

Thunderous gunfire erupted in front of the building.

At the same time, the rest of the coordinated attack began. A truck crashed into the security gatehouse by the entrance to the parking garage. The SOG deputies posted in front of the federal courthouse across the street were swarmed. A van exploded on the corner of the San Diego Police Department one mile away. Perched on the hotel rooftop diagonal to the US Marshals' building, a sniper took aim with a high-powered semiautomatic Barrett M82 .50 caliber rifle that was going to pack one hell of a punch. He let loose on the tinted, bullet-resistant windows of the third floor using black tips—armor-piercing rounds.

None of this would kill the target. None of this was intended to kill her.

It was all a distraction.

As the guards in the lobby ran to assist the tactical deputies out front of the US Marshals' building, Belladonna took her messenger bag that hadn't been fully searched, leaving the main compartment open, and headed for the stairs.

The elevators were about to fill up and she wanted to avoid the crowd.

According to their protocol, every available SOG member and deputy trained for field duty was mobilizing to assist team members under direct fire outside: in front of the building, at the parking garage and by the courthouse. It would bleed them dry, leaving none inside.

The remaining personnel on the third floor, mostly analysts, IT and management, were moving to the conference room away from the windows. Huddled together where someone could eliminate several birdies with one stone.

For a witness, the procedure was different. They were to be isolated with a deputy in a holding room that had reinforced walls. The door could only be opened using a personal identification number.

Belladonna drew a deep breath, opened the stairwell door and walked onto the third floor. Her sniper was peppering the office space with high-caliber bullets meant to tear through armor. Making a beeline for the conference room, she unzipped a compartment on the side of the bag and removed a canister of halothane.

She hurried to the room and opened the glass door. Catching Will Draper's surprised gaze, she pulled the pin, dropped the canister and shut them in. The effect of the colorless, sweet-smelling sleeping agent was almost immediate, neutralizing fifteen people in a snap.

Turning on her heel, she marched toward the holding room. As soon as her sniper was out of ammo and McKenna had been baited and hooked by the lull in gunfire, she'd make her move.

Chapter Seventeen

Inside the holding room, Nick finally managed to get Lori to sit. He stood beside her, rubbing her back in small circles. Her body was taut with tension.

Even in the room with reinforced walls that reduced outside noise, it sounded like all hell was breaking loose.

The high-caliber rifle—a real humdinger of firepower—was still making mincemeat of the third floor. An explosion rocked the building, he gauged somewhere out front. There had also been reports of an attack at the parking garage and on tactical personnel stationed at the courthouse. Yaz, Charlie and all the others were properly swamped.

It was a war zone on multiple fronts. Damn. Had Belladonna mustered an army?

Lori was an hour from testifying. They'd gone through so much to keep her alive and get to this point, Nick wasn't going to let anything happen to her now.

The police would respond. SWAT would be on the scene to assist any minute. They were going to get through this.

Quiet fell, and Lori's shoulders relaxed. The fusillade of semiautomatic gunfire had stopped. Maybe it was over, or being handled by SWAT.

The police were less than a mile away. They had to be here by now.

A series of beeps resounded in the hall. Someone was probably coming to give them the all clear.

The door opened and Nick's blood turned to slush.

Even with the blond wig and stodgy suit, he recognized Belladonna in the flesh.

As he went to draw his Glock from the shoulder rig, she tossed a black bag on the table and lunged for him.

Her elbow caught him in the cheekbone, twisting his head to the side and sending pain grinding down his face and into his teeth.

Lori gasped, hopping up and scrambling back against the wall.

With a lightning move, Belladonna torqued his gun hand, threw a knee to his gut and disarmed him. His weapon clattered to the floor. In the struggle, he reached out to grab her, but only ended up with a handful of the wig and ripped it from her head.

She launched a fist at his windpipe, stealing his breath. But he managed to throw a quick jab to her face.

Belladonna reeled back into a reverse flip. Her rising feet, coming up like pistons, caught him square in the chin, snapping his head up. Momentum threw him backward into the wall.

Nick took a ragged breath, marveling at how badly he'd underestimated Belladonna's fighting skills. She landed softly on the balls of her feet, whipping out a left hook at his head.

A raw-numb tingling exploded in his eye, leaving him dazed. Instinct kept him moving and blocking. Belladonna pressed her advantage, unleashing a blitzkrieg of punches and kicks.

Somehow, he shoved her off, gaining space to defend himself.

They hammered each other with bare-knuckle blasts. Nick outweighed her and had more force behind his blows. But she was faster and better trained at hand-to-hand. He wouldn't last much longer before she trapped him in some deadly grip. Broke his arm. Snapped his neck.

Then that would be the endgame.

Getting to his gun was the only answer.

He spotted it under the table. Flinging a chair at her, he dove for it, his fingertips grazing the handle before Belladonna drove a heel into his kidneys and sent the gun skittering.

Nick's back throbbed where he'd been kicked. His eyes watered from the blow.

Lori made a play for the gun, the floral dress fluttering around her legs. Nick pushed up from the floor.

Belladonna was a blur of movement, rolling across the table.

Lori grabbed the gun and lifted it to fire. But the assassin kicked it from her grasp and sent it flying in the air.

As Nick jumped up and to the side for the weapon, Belladonna whirled, snatching Lori.

They faced each other in a standoff, panting.

Nick had the gun, safety off, finger on the trigger. And Belladonna had Lori positioned in front of her like a human shield and a dagger-sharp hairpin to Lori's throat. The assassin's black hair had tumbled loose, falling freely, almost curtaining what little of her face was exposed.

Belladonna pressed the pointed tip of the deadly instrument to Lori's carotid artery.

Nick made eye contact with Lori. Her face was stark with fear.

Panic swelled in his chest. He held the gun rock steady, but he didn't have a clear shot.

He shifted his gaze to the assassin. "Kill her and I kill you." He issued the imperative statement of fact without letting the fear flooding him leak into his voice, his tone glacial.

"I know." The utter lack of concern from Belladonna sent a trickle of cold sweat down Nick's spine. Then she said, "But I don't want to die today. I have a proposal."

It was some kind of trick, had to be. "I'm just supposed to trust that, after you've relentlessly pursued us with every intention of ending both our lives?"

"I used halothane on the people in the conference room. I could've used it on you two instead. Once you were out cold, I could've killed Lori and fled."

Nick narrowed his eyes at her. "Then why didn't you?"

"My personal circumstances have changed. I have one chance to break free of Dante Vargas. And this is it, but I need your help."

His heart stuttered at the turnabout. "What? You're insane if you think I'm going to help you."

"I have a family and he's threatened their lives unless I kill her." Belladonna nudged the sharp tip against Lori's throat, drawing a drop of blood.

Starbursts of red exploded behind his eyes, and he clenched the gun tighter, praying for enough clearance between the two women to put a bullet in Belladonna's head.

"Dante has promised to release me from his service if I follow through, but he is the prince of lies," Belladonna said. "He'll never free me. And if I don't get out, then one day, he'll claim my daughter, too. I can't let that happen. So I have a proposal. One where we both win."

"You made several attempts on my life, her life," Nick said through clenched teeth. "Who knows how many good people are dying right now under the siege you started outside? And you've already murdered one deputy at our safe house. I don't see a scenario where we can both win."

Mentally, he sifted through options, his mind scrambling to think of a way to get Lori through this alive. Even if he signaled Lori to take some action, throw an elbow back into Belladonna, anything to get distance between them so he could get a shot, it wouldn't work.

Belladonna wasn't flush to Lori, leaving her ribs exposed to an attack. She stood at an angle as if anticipating some countermove.

"Lucky for us both, I do," Belladonna said. "Lori lives and testifies. That's the win you want. I leave, you put the word out that a female suspect meeting my description was killed making an attempt on her life, and I give you the name of your traitor. That's the win I want. You should want that, too."

"I know who the traitor is. Will Draper."

"Really?" Her granite expression shifted. "Do you have proof?" A ghost of a smile stretched across Belladonna's tight face. "I do. Look in my bag. Middle compartment."

Nick kept the gun raised and backpedaled to the table. Not taking his eyes off Belladonna, he felt for the compartment. It was open. He pulled out a laptop.

"Do you recognize the serial number?" she asked.

His gaze bounced between the assassin and the computer. He turned it over and checked the number. His blood turned cold.

Belladonna flipped open the badge hanging around her neck, showing him the ID. "Your traitor is Ted Zeeman. Not Will Draper."

His mind reeled, the breath in his lungs stalled. "We have Ted's body in the morgue."

"No. The body you have in the morgue was planted in your safe house by one of my people. On the laptop, I've downloaded Ted's dental records and the records for the person in the morgue."

Nick shook his head in disbelief, blowing out a shaky breath.

"Who do you want more? Me, someone who is being coerced and threatened? Or Ted Zeeman? Someone you trusted, who betrayed you for money. The morning of your trip to the mall, Ted gave me the address to the safe house and left his badge and laptop for one of my people in the trash bin outside. When the attempt at the mall failed, he called me from a convenience store to find out the contingency plan. He let you walk into that house, thinking neither of you would be walking back out.

"We used his laptop to breach your system. Dante Vargas has the WITSEC list and the names of every deputy marshal. Ted facilitated that. He's the one who put a roving bug on your cell phone for me, so I could not only track you but also listen to all your calls. He also gave me the details about your protocol and procedures. How do you think I was able to get in here? Whose PIN do you think I used to open that door?"

Fury beat in Nick's chest like the wings of a startled bird. "You know where Ted is?"

"Yes. I arranged his transportation out of the country and can tell you exactly where to find him, a beautiful white sand beach. I want Lori to live. I want her to testify, to hurt Vargas and the cartel. I also want to disappear with my family. So I'll ask you again. Who do you want more? Me? Or backstabbing Ted?"

If he had to make a choice, there was no contest. This was personal. He wanted to rip Ted's head off.

"A draw is a good thing," Belladonna said with that silver tongue, in her honeyed voice. "No more bloodshed. I'll stop the siege outside."

And he could end the assault going on outside, possibly save lives? It was the only choice. "Deal."

"Put your gun on the floor. Kick it away and I'll release her."

Belladonna could've used halothane on them, killed Lori and left. But she hadn't because maybe her story about her family and wanting freedom from Vargas was true. Nick did as she instructed and raised his palms.

"If Will Draper gives you a hard time about going along with our deal and my death isn't reported in the news as we've agreed, tell that bastard I'll come for him and I promise he'll die screaming."

Nick nodded. He was okay with that.

"Ted is in the Maldives. I downloaded his address and imagery of the island onto the laptop, as well."

"How did you know how this was going to play out? That I'd agree?"

"It's a talent of mine." She punched in the code, unlocking the door, and opened it.

Releasing Lori, Belladonna touched her ear. That was when he spotted the comms device.

"Echo Sierra," she said, letting the door close.

Nick grabbed his gun, contemplating going after her. A second later the power was cut, trapping them inside the room. Effectively eliminating that option.

In the darkness, Nick found Lori and hauled her into his arms. "When she had you with that spike to your throat, I died a thousand deaths."

He felt her tears on his cheeks. Then again, he couldn't be certain he wasn't the one crying. Gratitude and relief tangled through him and he squeezed her tighter, not wanting to ever let her go.

The power came back and he stared at Lori in the light. Her eyes were glassy and her face damp. He cupped her cheeks and pressed his forehead to hers.

"Oh, God," she said on a catch of breath. Lori nestled closer, her fingers clutching his back. "I wasn't ready. For this to be it."

"I know." He kissed her lips, tasting the salt of their mingled tears. The thought of her coming so close to death still made his heart contract.

"You saved my life again." Her voice was rough with emotion.

"Didn't really have much choice. That's the job."

She laughed and cried at the same time. "Stop saying that."

"Okay." He wiped away her tears with his thumb. "You're more than a witness to me. You have been for months. I can't say exactly when it happened, but I'm so in love with you that—"

Beeps chimed in the hall.

Nick and Lori pulled apart but stayed close.

The holding room door opened, and Yazzie crossed the threshold, eyeing them both. "You two are both okay, good. Charlie is helping the others in the conference room. They were hit with some kind of sleeping gas, but they're waking up." His voice was hesitant as his gaze flickered between them like he was picking up on their energy. "The attacks stopped. They just pulled back and left. The police are in pursuit."

"I gathered," Nick said. "We lose anyone?"

"No. Lots of injuries, but everyone is going to live. Draper is conscious. He wants eyes on the witness right now."

"Yeah, okay. I need to talk to him anyway. There have been some developments."

TESTIFYING HAD LIFTED a great load from Lori's shoulders. But when new marshals waited for her outside the courtroom, the weight was quickly replaced by a different strain.

"Can you give us one minute?" Nick asked the deputies there to relocate her.

They both nodded and stepped a few feet away.

Keeping her alive, getting her on the stand, was always going to lead here, but she hadn't had time to think about it. Until now.

"They won't tell me where you're going," he said low. "Protocol." He slipped her a piece of paper, his fingertips brushing hers, lingering. "When you're able to, provided you want to, call me."

She'd spent every day with this man for a year and didn't even know his phone number. Something about that made her heart ache. "Of course I want to. I will as soon as I can."

"I won't be able to come to you right away. It'll be a little while before I can see you."

Her chest tightened. "Why?"

One of the deputies waiting leveled a reproving glance at them, and he dropped his hand from hers.

"I'm on a plane to the Maldives tomorrow. We don't have an extradition treaty with them, but Draper doesn't give a damn any more than I do. I'm going to bring Ted back and he's going to answer for what he's done."

"Is Draper going to honor Belladonna's request?" She discreetly tucked his phone number in her bra.

Nick nodded, a ghost of a smile on his lips. "It didn't take much convincing after I passed along Belladonna's message."

"Once you bring Ted back, you'll come to see me?"

Nick glanced over at the deputies coming toward them. "No. I need to wait until they have you settled and back off. A few weeks at most. I swear."

Earnestness gleamed in his whiskey-brown eyes and echoed in his words.

"McKenna, we can't give you any longer. The SOG unit is waiting to escort us to make sure we don't run into any problems along the way."

"Okay," Nick said, taking a step back, his brow creased. "Lori...*kharabetam*."

She knew the word was Farsi but didn't have a clue what it meant.

With a deputy positioned on either side of her, Lori put one foot in front of the other and walked away from the only man she'd ever truly loved.

Each step she took deepened the ache swelling in her chest. A torrent of emotions whirled through her and she didn't know how much more upheaval she could handle before falling apart. And for the next few weeks, she'd have to hold it together without Nick.

Nick.

Lori spun around, breaking away from the deputies, ignoring their questions, and ran back to Nick. She stopped short of grabbing him and kissing him and making an even bigger spectacle. "*Kharabetam.* What does it mean?"

He gave her a warm smile, his eyes radiating love. "I'll tell you the next time we're face-to-face and I'm free to kiss you."

"You sure do know how to leave a woman hanging."

"Well, I've got to keep you thinking about me someway."

"Trust me. No effort at all on your part is required."

One of the deputies took her by the elbow, and they escorted her away.

Epilogue

Nick had found Ted Zeeman seated on a powdery white sand beach beside a hut, fishing, drinking beer and canoodling with a woman.

His female companion had been a surprise. A prostitute he'd fallen for who happened to work for *Los Chacales*. The cartel controlled much of the prostitution in California, so it was only two degrees of separation.

Pillow talk had been Ted's undoing. After a particularly glorious evening, he'd let it slip that he'd be out of town for a year, guarding a high-profile witness for the big WCM case. He'd arranged to meet his lady friend in a motel near Big Bear to have his pipes cleaned every three months. Turned out the cartel offered money for information about Lori's whereabouts. Every month, the bait for a tip had increased. Once it had gotten to a ridiculous sum, the woman blabbed.

At his last scheduled rendezvous, Belladonna had been waiting for Ted.

Zeeman had offered the confidential laptop, his credentials and information about the marshal's protocol in exchange for Belladonna giving him a clean exit strategy.

Slapping handcuffs on Ted had been ten times more satisfying than Nick had imagined.

But absolutely nothing topped this moment. Standing under the warm Phoenix sunshine in front of Lori's apartment door. Her last name was Washington now, but one day he'd hoped to make it McKenna.

Nick knocked, excitement buzzing in his veins.

Lori opened the door and his world righted.

Her hair had been lightened to the color of melted caramel, doe eyes sparkling in the light, gorgeous in a form-fitting white sundress that clung to her curves like a second skin.

She was a sight for sore eyes that immediately got him hard and set his heart on fire.

He silently promised he'd be a gentleman and not pounce on her until after lunch.

Lori launched herself at him, wrapping her legs around his waist, and kissed him.

He supported her weight with an arm beneath her rear and carried her inside, kicking the door shut behind them.

After dropping his suitcase, he curled his fingers in her hair and deepened the kiss.

She was vibrantly alive in his arms. Her lips were petal smooth, her tongue coaxing.

"You smell so good, feel so good," he said in a rough whisper. "You're making it tough for me to be a gentleman."

"How about you be the natural hellion that you are and make love to me until I can't remember my new last name?"

"Happy to oblige."

He pressed her back against the wall and tore open

the front of her dress, sending tiny pearl buttons skittering to the floor.

No underwear. *Oh, man.*

There was only creamy bare skin inviting him to touch and play. He kissed and licked and nibbled her neck, over the faint line from her old wound, down to her breasts. Sucked on her nipple.

Arousal kicked him hard, his skin tightening with anticipation at the pleasure that awaited them both.

She unfastened his belt, lowered his zipper and grinned at his rock-hard erection. "Have I told you how impressive you are?"

"No, but feel free."

Her hand closed over him and squeezed, spurring him to shamelessly moan.

He cupped her sex, finding her hot and wet and equally ready. "Condoms are in my bag," he said, proud of himself for remembering.

"Can't wait. Been thinking about this for days." She positioned him precisely where she wanted him. "I need you now."

Their union was quick but all-consuming. Urgency drove each unrestrained thrust. They moved as one, stroking and groping, their coupling of love and lust. Need gathered fast, painful as a bruise. It was wild and mindless, but achingly beautiful.

Shoving his hand down between them, he circled the right button, making sure they came together. The world turned stark white as pleasure shot through him hotter than a bullet. Her scream of satisfaction filled his ears, and he couldn't help but smile.

He carried her to the sofa, more of a shuffle, really, with his pants around his ankles. Thankfully, it was a short distance. They dropped in a tangle, still connected. He soaked up the contact, the sweet brew of sensation, like a greedy sponge.

She ran her fingers through his hair and tugged his head back, meeting his gaze. "I've waited five hundred and…" She looked at the clock on the wall. "And thirty-five hours to know. What does *kharabetam* mean?"

He gave her a deep, soul-wrenching kiss. "It literally means I'm ruined for you." Cupping her face, he brushed his thumb over her cheek.

Happy tears glistened in her eyes. "Good, because you're stuck with me."

He laughed, stroking her hair. "Do you like living in Phoenix?"

She shrugged. "It's okay. Better than backcountry nowhere."

"I'm going to put in for a transfer, but before I do, I wanted to see if you were open to moving."

"I'd love to. It's not as if I've found a job yet, but can I?"

"Sure, as long as it's not a city you've lived in before or have family. I was thinking about Vegas."

A bright smile spread across her face. "Yes!" she squealed with absolute delight. "I love your family and it would be amazing to be close to them."

"There are some bounty hunters I know who could use an office manager. Someone capable of balancing the books. Interested?"

"Of course."

"And I was thinking, maybe we could get married, next year. In the spring. Mom says the weather is perfect for a wedding."

Her eyes grew wide and she looked choked up.

Way to go for moving too fast. "We can take it slower if you like. I didn't mean to rush you."

"You're not. It's just that you're giving me everything I've ever dreamed about and hoped for, making wishes I didn't even know I had come true."

His heart rolled over in his chest. "I love you, Lori. I want to give you the world. I want you to be the mother of my children and grow old with you. I really am ruined for you."

"Ditto, *kharabetam*."

"Now, I've got a really big question for you."

"Bigger than me moving and marrying you?"

"In a way, yes. How do you feel about me taking you on a proper date? We've never had one."

Her smile blossomed, growing wider and deeper and filling him with the loveliest sensation he'd ever known. He would do anything for this woman.

She brushed her lips against his, soft and sweet, and said, "I thought you'd never ask."

His cell phone rang, and he was tempted to ignore it, but she fished it out of his pocket and handed it to him.

He answered without looking at the caller ID. "This better be good."

"It's me, Charlie. Aiden and I are in a world of trouble. We need your help."

Why couldn't they have waited to call after his first date with Lori?

Nick sighed. "What do you need?"

* * * * *

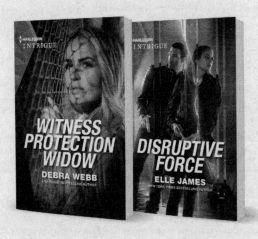

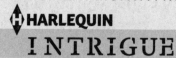

Available April 21, 2020

#1923 SECRET INVESTIGATION
Tactical Crime Division • by Elizabeth Heiter
When battle armor inexplicably fails and soldiers perish, the Tactical Crime Division springs into action. With the help of Petrov Armor CEO Leila Petrov, can undercover agent Davis Rogers discover secrets larger than anyone ever imagined?

#1924 CONARD COUNTY JUSTICE
Conard County: The Next Generation • by Rachel Lee
Major Daniel Duke will do whatever it takes to catch his brother's killer, but Deputy Cat Jansen is worried that he'll hinder her investigation. As the stakes increase, they must learn to work together to find the murderer. If they can't, they could pay with their lives...

#1925 WHAT SHE KNEW
Rushing Creek Crime Spree • by Barb Han
When a baby appears on navy SEAL Rylan Anderson's doorstep, he enlists old friend Amber Kent for help. But when the child is nearly abducted in Amber's care, they realize they must discover the truth behind the baby's identity in order to stop the people trying to kidnap her.

#1926 BACKCOUNTRY ESCAPE
A Badlands Cops Novel • by Nicole Helm
Felicity Harrison is being framed for murder. Family friend Gage Wyatt vows to keep her safe until they find the real culprit, but there's a killer out there who doesn't just want Felicity framed—but silenced for good.

#1927 THE HUNTING SEASON
by Janice Kay Johnson
After a string of murders connected to CPS social worker Lindsay Eagle's caseload is discovered, Detective Daniel Deperro is placed on protective detail. But Lindsay won't back down from the investigation, even as Daniel fears she's the next target. Will his twenty-four-hour protection enrage the killer further?

#1928 MURDER IN THE SHALLOWS
by Debbie Herbert
When a routine patrol sets Bailey Covington on the trail of a serial killer, the reclusive park ranger joins forces with sheriff's deputy Dylan Armstrong. Bailey can't forgive Dylan's family for betraying her, but they'll have to trust each other find two missing women before a murderer strikes again.

YOU CAN FIND MORE INFORMATION ON UPCOMING HARLEQUIN TITLE FREE EXCERPTS AND MORE AT HARLEQUIN.COM.

She wiped up stray crumbs, then tried to smile at him. "Coffee?"

"I've intruded too much."

She put a hand on her hip. "I might have thought so earlier, but I'm not feeling that way now. This is important. I give a damn about Larry, and now I give a damn about you. You might not want it, but I care. So quiet down. Coffee? Or something else?"

"A beer if you have another."

As it happened, she did. "I buy this so rarely that you're in luck."

"Then why did you buy it?"

"Larry," she answered simply.

For the first time, they shared a look of real understanding. The sense of connection warmed her.

She hadn't expected to feel this way, not when it came to Duke. Maybe it helped to realize he wasn't just a monolith of anger and unswaying determination.

As Cat returned to her seat, she said, "You put me off initially."

Another half smile from him. "I never would have guessed."

A laugh escaped her, brief but genuine. "I'm usually better at concealing my reactions to people. But there you were, looking like a battering ram. You sure looked hard and angry. Nothing about you made me want to get into a tussle."

He looked at the beer bottle he held. "Most people don't want to tangle with me. I can understand your reaction. I came through that door loaded for bear. Too much time to think on the way here, maybe."

"You looked like walking death," she told him frankly. "An icy-cold fury. Worse, in my opinion, than a heated rage. Scary."

"Comes with the territory," he said after a moment, then took a swig of his beer.

She could probably wonder until the cows came home exactly what he meant by that. Maybe it was better not to know.

Don't miss
Conard County Justice *by Rachel Lee,*
available May 2020 wherever
Harlequin Intrigue books and ebooks are sold.

Harlequin.com

Get 4 FREE REWARDS!

We'll send you 2 FREE Books plus 2 FREE Mystery Gifts.

Harlequin Intrigue books are action-packed stories that will keep you on the edge of your seat. Solve the crime and deliver justice at all costs.

FREE
Value Over
$20

YES! Please send me 2 FREE Harlequin Intrigue novels and my 2 FREE gifts (gifts are worth about $10 retail). After receiving them, if I don't wish to receive any more books, I can return the shipping statement marked "cancel." If I don't cancel, I will receive 6 brand-new novels every month and be billed just $4.99 each for the regular-print edition or $5.99 each for the larger-print edition in the U.S., or $5.74 each for the regular-print edition or $6.49 each for the larger-print edition in Canada. That's a savings of at least 12% off the cover price! It's quite a bargain! Shipping and handling is just 50¢ per book in the U.S. and $1.25 per book in Canada.* I understand that accepting the 2 free books and gifts places me under no obligation to buy anything. I can always return a shipment and cancel at any time. The free books and gifts are mine to keep no matter what I decide.

Choose one: ☐ **Harlequin Intrigue**
Regular-Print
(182/382 HDN GNXC)

☐ **Harlequin Intrigue**
Larger-Print
(199/399 HDN GNXC)

Name (please print)

Address   Apt. #

City   State/Province   Zip/Postal Code

Mail to the **Reader Service:**
IN U.S.A.: P.O. Box 1341, Buffalo, NY 14240-8531
IN CANADA: P.O. Box 603, Fort Erie, Ontario L2A 5X3

Want to try 2 free books from another series? Call 1-800-873-8635 or visit www.ReaderService.com.

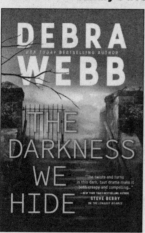

SPECIAL EXCERPT FROM

*Dr. Rowan Dupont and police chief Billy Brannigan
have one final opportunity to catch dangerous serial
killer Julian Addington, but will their teamwork be
enough to stop him—or will he find them first?*

Read on for a sneak preview of
The Darkness We Hide
by USA TODAY bestselling author Debra Webb.

Winchester, Tennessee
Monday, March 9, 7:35 a.m.

Rowan Dupont parked on the southeast side of the
downtown square. The county courthouse sat smack in the
middle of Winchester with streets forming a grid around it.
Shops, including a vintage movie theater, revitalized over
the past few years by local artisans, lined the sidewalks.
Something Rowan loved most about her hometown were the
beautiful old trees that still stood above all else. So often the
trees were the first things to go when towns received a face-
lift. Not in Winchester. The entire square had been refreshed
and the majestic old trees still stood.

This morning the promise of spring was impossible to
miss. Blooms and leaves sprouted from every bare limb.
This was her favorite time of year. A new beginning.
Anything could happen.

Rowan sighed. Funny how being back in Winchester had
come to mean so much to her these past several months. As a
teenager she couldn't wait to get away from home. Growing

up in a funeral home had made her different from the other kids. She was the daughter of the undertaker, a curiosity. At twelve tragedy had struck and she'd lost her twin sister and her mother within months of each other. The painful events had driven her to the very edge. By the time she'd finished high school, she was beyond ready for a change of scenery. Despite having spent more than twenty years living in the big city hiding from the memories of home and a dozen of those two decades working with Nashville's police department—in Homicide, no less—she had been forced to see that there was no running away. No hiding from the secrets of her past.

There were too many secrets, too many lies, to be ignored.

Yet despite all that had happened the first eighteen years of her life, she was immensely glad to be back home.

If only the most painful part of her time in Nashville— serial killer Julian Addington—hadn't followed her home and wreaked havoc those first months after her return.

Rowan took a breath and emerged from her SUV. The morning air was brisk and fresh. More glimpses of spring's impending arrival showed in pots overflowing with tulips, daffodils and crocuses. Those same early bloomers dotted the landscape beds all around the square. It was a new year and she was very grateful to have the previous year behind her.

She might not be able to change the past, but she could forge a different future, and she intended to do exactly that.

Don't miss
The Darkness We Hide *by Debra Webb,*
available April 2020 wherever
MIRA books and ebooks are sold.

Harlequin.com